In the Shadow of the Bayonet

Chris Boult

First published in Great Britain by Pen Press

All paper used in the printing of this book has been made from
wood grown in managed, sustainable forests.

ISBN13: 978-1-78003-761-5

Printed and bound in the UK
Pen Press is an imprint of
Indepenpress Publishing Limited
25 Eastern Place
Brighton
BN2 1GJ

A catalogue record of this book is available from
the British Library

Cover design by Jacqueline Abromeit

In Memory of

Lance Corporal Stephen Anderson,
The Staffordshire Regiment

Who died too young and missed too much.

About the Author

Chris is still a serving probation officer, with over 30 years' experience in social work and criminal justice. He trained in Nottingham in the 1970's and early 80's, worked briefly in two different Social Services Departments and served in the Army in East Midlands  Universities Officer Training Corps, with The Mercian Volunteers and completed a short service commission in the Staffordshire Regiment before joining Staffordshire Probation Service in 1986. He now has over 27 years' experience in probation including 17 years as a manager at various levels and settings. He has worked largely with high risk offenders, in both prison and the community, and has extensive experience of multi-agency work including MAPPA. He has an interest in programmes, and is a qualified trainer.

In 2008 at age 50, he decided to move on from management and return to practice. He has worked in a prison setting, report writing and as an Offender Supervisor in both the private and public sectors. He now works part-time in a women's prison.

In developing his interest in training, Chris has written and delivered training and is a visiting lecturer at Staffordshire University.

Since going part time Chris has developed some business interests and latterly indulged a long held ambition to write a book.

In the Shadow of the Bayonet is his first novel. A sequel is already under way and he has further ideas for more books to come.

Glossary of terms

2IC	Second in command
Bergen	Military rucksack
ERV/ RV	Emergency/ rendezvous
Cat A	Category A high security prison
CO	Commanding officer
Collateral damage	Military term for unintended civilian casualties
CJ	Criminal justice
CJS	Criminal justice system
Crap hats	Military derogatory term for soldiers serving outside Special Forces
CSM	Company Sergeant Major
Decompression	Period of recuperation post operational tour
DCI	Detective Chief Inspector
Indeterminate sentence	Prison sentence with open ended release date
Lifer	Life sentence prisoner
MAPPA	Multi Agency Public Protection Arrangements
MO	Medical officer
NATO	North Atlantic treaty organisation
NCO	Non commissioned officer
No 2 dress	Formal military uniform
OC	Officer commanding/ in charge
P Company	Parachute regiment selection

People Trafficking	
	Illegal movement of people for profit
POPO	Prolific and priority offenders
PTSD	Post traumatic stress disorder
QM	Quarter master
REME	Royal electrical and mechanical engineers
RSM	Regimental Sergeant Major
Rupert	Slang term for young officer
Rupert factory	Royal military academy Sandhurst
Section	Eight man infantry fighting unit
SOPS	Standard operating procedures
Squaddies	Slang term for soldiers
Tariff	Minimum term of a life sentence to be served in custody

Preface

I wish to acknowledge the part played by public servants everywhere, especially those working in criminal justice and our armed forces, whose efforts often go unrecognised and uncelebrated.

This novel is set in the summer of 2013.

I wish to make it clear that although it follows events at the time, it is not, nor was it intended to be wholly historically accurate. I have deliberately avoided too close a reference to actual places but the action takes place along the southern coast of Cyprus in the region of the military base. Also, that whilst the characters are based on perceptions of plausibility, they are not related to any known individuals and any unintended similarity is therefore entirely coincidental, for which I apologise in advance.

Any opinions expressed here are entirely my own and are not intended to be, nor are they in any way the official doctrine of the agencies alluded to.

Chapter 1

John Dalton sat in The Beach Bar at Blue Bay on the North West coast of Cyprus, gently sipping an ice cold local beer, reflecting on his career and his life. He wondered about the future. There were uncertainties, but also hopes.

John had just retired three months ago and moved to Cyprus. What an opportunity! He was looking forward to unwinding in the hills and the fresh air. He had always enjoyed walking by the sea and Cyprus had so many beaches to explore. He was excited. His only reservation had been that he had left behind so many friends and as a single man he thought he might be lonely. John was a sociable man, so he didn't lack confidence but never the less the prospect of finding a whole set of new friends, contacts and acquaintances was a little unnerving. He was however determined to make this work. After a full working life John didn't regard the prospect of overuse of an armchair particularly appealing and the thought of day time television was anathema.

John had worked as a probation officer for 30 years. He had enjoyed an interesting career working in different parts of England. Trying to strike a balance between government policy, protecting the public and looking after the needs of the offender had always had its challenges. John had worked in the community, in prisons and in hostels. He had never sought promotion, regarding the job as a public service and the real work being done on the ground dealing face to face with offenders. Would he miss the politics, the constant change, the pressure? He very much doubted it!

He had woken to a fine morning with the promise of unbroken sunshine to come. The sea gently rolled onto the shore with the characteristic reassuring and soothing sound of Mediterranean waves announcing their arrival on warm sand. The scene was a constant invitation to relax. Here there seemed no need to rush or to tackle six projects all at once. John thought how good it felt to have left behind that ever more pressurised life back in England. Here the culture was different, the people were more relaxed and of course the weather was a constant bonus!

John had looked at different accommodation options when planning his move and bought a modest apartment, suitable for his needs. He had briefly met some of the neighbours and talked to locals and ex pats in the nearby shops and bars. He hadn't as yet found someone he would call a friend however.

****

Paul Tryba strode confidently across the beach with Hash at his side, a 3 year old black Labrador cross, who was his constant companion. He chuckled to himself as he savoured the contrast with his previous life. Shifts, conflict, politics, ever changing goal posts, depravity and tragedy ran through his mind as he walked barefoot across the sand. Paul liked the international feel of the island. His father was Polish and had settled in England after the Second World War. His father always spoke very fondly of the English for the welcome and assistance he had received as an immigrant at that time. Attitudes had hardened since, but after the war there was a greater sense of communal struggle; whoever you were or wherever you came from. As had happened following the First World War, social barriers had started to be eroded.

Paul had moved to Cyprus a year ago. Well laid and much looked forward to plans had not worked out as well as expected. Having retired and moved abroad, he had not envisaged being alone quite so soon.

He saw the sun glint off the roof of The Beach Bar and felt the draw of its appeal. In no hurry, he veered towards the steps calling Hash to heel. Hash needed a drink and so did he. Hash sniffed around the decking, seeking the familiar water bowl that she new was there to be found. John looked up, seeing the dog and signalled that it was OK to approach in a way that dogs and humans both seem to understand. Hash responded, enjoying the fuss and attention from an unexpected source.

After exchanging the pleasantries that dogs often precipitate, Paul asked if he could join the stranger. 'Yes, sure,' John said as Paul took a seat. 'Lovely morning isn't it?'

The two men seemed to instinctively know that there was a connection between them.

As the conversation developed both were trying to avoid it but knew inevitably that one or other would succumb to curiosity, as Paul eventually asked 'What brings you here?' and the conversation started to unwrap their respective lives.

'You sound like you're from the UK; have you retired here too?' enquired John.

'Yes, I've been here a year.'

'Has it worked out for you? Do you like it?'

'I do like it, yes, but it has not quite been as I expected.' Paul explained about the sudden death of his wife Sandra from cancer. 'It's been hard on my own. I hadn't expected to face building a new life without Sandra so soon after arriving here. Work and family have been my life and now the family has grown and I've left work behind. After all those years of longing for this stage in my life, it hasn't been what I thought it would be. I wonder should we have made even more effort to enjoy life along the way; more so than we did?'

'I'm sorry to hear that. I'm single. I never married, but it must be very hard to loose your wife at this stage in your life, but it's no good having regrets.'

'No, you are right, but it's difficult.'

'Yes of course. What did you do, were you in the people business?' asked John, suspecting that he was.

'Funny you should say that, but I suppose I was. I worked as a prison officer in different prisons and finished my career in West Wood open prison in Dorset. I'd always dreamt of moving to Cyprus and of walking in warm sunshine. During my last years at work I would walk with my dog Hash on a nearby beach.....and you?'

'Believe it or not I was a probation officer.'

The two men laughed at the irony of striking up a conversation seemingly with a stranger at random only to find such a connection.

Paul and Sandra had always worked hard and Paul had tried to balance work with some modest enjoyment along the way, with holidays and hobbies. He was grateful that they had done so as their time together had been cruelly cut short. He remained haunted however that he had not done enough. He reflected on his time as a prison officer; he had seen attitudes and prison conditions change considerably. Like many of his colleagues he had some sympathy with the view that the service had lost sight of who was the 'offender'. Modern prisons offered such good conditions and facilities that they rivalled many a university campus. Hardly a deterrent, let alone best use of public money compared with other needs like hospitals and schools. On the other hand experience of seeing the same offenders return time and time again to prison suggested that something was wrong with the system and sometimes he thought sentencing had gone too far in placating 'the hang 'em and flog 'em Brigade', when a bit of help and a leg up would be more appropriate. With some of the people he'd dealt with over the years it was difficult to avoid the conclusion that they were doomed from the moment of conception and never had a chance.

Another man walked into the bar, struck up a conversation with the owner, ordered a drink and sat out on the decking looking out to sea. He had a certain bearing about him, suggesting having spent at least some time in uniform. He sat at the bar talking to the tourist next to him who was French. They shared their experiences of foreign travel as Hash looked around the bar for interesting things to explore. The Frenchman was about to leave when Mike heard the sound of English voices across the room. The tone sounded somehow familiar. He half listened for a while as he drank his coffee, then decided to satisfy his curiosity and walked over towards the other two men. 'Is this Brit corner?' he enquired as he approached the table where John and Paul sat.

'Yeah, pull up a chair mate. I'm Paul, this is John.'

'Mike; pleased to meet you.'

As the three men got talking, the criminal justice connection between all three of them soon became apparent. Mike had recently retired from the police as a Detective Chief Inspector. They laughed at finding themselves in Cyprus sitting in a bar in the sun, but still talking about the seedy side of life that all of them were familiar with in their previous professional lives. There was an obvious and immediate rapport between them as they readily enjoyed the conversation and each others' company.

'So what made you leave the police then, Mike?' John asked.

Mike explained that he had left the police early when the force had to reduce numbers to meet government cuts. Senior officers had always had reservations about this approach, depleting so much expertise and experience at one time, but government just wanted to save money.

'A career in the police was traditionally regarded as a profession in which you could start young and finish early given the physical nature of the job. I had always looked forward to this so took the opportunity to retire when it arose, although with twins at university I had hoped to work a little longer to support them financially,' Mike explained.

After a while the conversation paused and Paul took the initiative.

'Well guys, I fancy a walk back along the beach, Hash is getting restless. Would you like to join me?' The others had nothing planned so the invitation seemed like a natural extension of their conversation.

Over the days that followed the three men quickly formed a bond based on shared experience. They found themselves in the same place and the same time at the same stage in their respective lives. They met in the bars and the coffee shops, walked on the beach with Hash and enjoyed exchanging stories about their working lives and holding informal debates on issues from their experience in criminal justice. One of them would start on a theme and the others could immediately relate to it and add to the rich pool of commentary on humanity in all its rawness. They also started to share their personal thoughts and feelings on life and love and beer.

On this particular Thursday morning Paul was feeling especially sad and irritable. He was struggling to resist feeling angry, bitter and resentful about his situation. He had worked hard all his life, looked forward to his retirement and now this. It was so unfair. He needed the company of others to help distract his attention. He called John but there was no reply. Was there anyone out there? Did anyone care? He wondered.

John came out of the shower and selected his usual clothes from a minimal selection. Do I really need more than two sets of flip flops, shorts and tee shirts in this climate, he argued. He checked his phone whilst the kettle boiled. He noticed the missed call from Paul and responded immediately without trying to retrieve any message, knowing that Paul would probably have lost patience with the technology very quickly when it failed to reply.

'Hi Paul, its John, you OK?'

'No, you miserable shit, I'm fucking not!'

'Oh dear, what's the problem?'

'It's Sandra; I can't get her out of my mind.'

'Hey, come on, that's hardly surprising, she's been a key part of your life for a long time, you will miss her…..'

'Key part, fucking key part, she was the only part that mattered!'

'I know….'

'You don't know! Don't patronise me!'

'OK,' John conceded, 'you obviously feel raw today. Come on, grab Hash, I'll talk to Mike and we can all meet at The Beach Bar for breakfast; how about that?'

'I'll be there', Paul replied.

Mike and John shared their concern and sympathy for Paul over the phone and set off for the arranged meeting.

'I'm sorry, John. I shouldn't have reacted like that. It's not your fault,' said Paul quickly as they arrived and took their seats and Mike ordered some coffee.

'Don't worry, it's no problem. It's hard, genuinely hard. But don't think we don't care or sympathise, because we do. We've all seen enough human suffering for three lifetimes. Life often isn't fair and can be cruel, but it's all we've got, so let's make the best of it.'

'That doesn't sound like a probation officer to me Paul, does it to you? Where did that come from?'

John had joined the probation service when probation officers were quite autonomous, where the ethos was to select the right people, train them well and give them the flexibility to use their discretion and professional judgment in getting on alongside offenders and trying to make a difference. 'Advise, Assist and Befriend' was the maxim. All this had started to change in the 1980's with the advent of 'Efficiency, Effectiveness and Economy.'

Government moved on from the vague and looking back on it slightly quaint view that worthy professionals could simply apply themselves to do their best with the attempt being justification enough in itself almost regardless of the impact and outcome. When questions started to be asked about consistency of practice, standards and expectations, effectiveness of one intervention over another and value for money, the probation service was found wanting. Little hard evidence or research existed and even a friendly and sympathetic observer could not avoid the conclusion that the service had to move on and address some of these questions more robustly.

'Where are all those long words and fancy jargon, John?'

'Yeah, sounds more like what I'd say a hundred times a day to prisoners, Mike......common sense….. Jargon, but if you want jargon, go to those bloody psychologists. We were flooded with them in the prison, all fresh from university with a degree in the bleeding obvious.'

Psychology by contrast to probation came from more of a scientific rather than a sociological tradition and found itself much better placed to fill the gap in the development of programmes to address offenders' behaviour. Such programmes were more consistent and well managed, monitored and researched and began to gain some credibility. If offenders generally tend to lack specific skills and attributes, then attempts to embody these in a systematic way had a logic. For example, offenders often do not plan their activities but respond impulsively to situations without thinking them through or considering the consequences. Therefore to offer programmes that develop skills in decision making, problem solving and consequential thinking, including the impact on others can make sense in trying to reduce crime and its negative impact on victims.

'OK Paul, take the piss by all means, but there is something in psychology; perspective taking, challenging irrational thoughts and positive thinking, for example.'

'Now that does sound more like a probation officer, eh Paul?'

The three laughed and recalled more stories as the sea rolled in. The coffee tasted good and Hash sat patiently waiting for the walk she trusted would follow.

'Come on, let's walk along a bit.' suggested Paul.

They moved off along the beach, enjoying the warm sunshine and the open space. Hash ran in circles, churning up the sand as she expressed her excitement in running wild and free. She threw a length of seaweed into the air, caught it and rolled over, before running straight into the sea and shaking water all over her unsuspecting master.

'What was it all about?' reflected Paul. 'Best part of a hundred years public service between us and was it appreciated, did we make a difference?'

'Well, we helped some of the people some of the time,' responded John.

'I made a difference taking some of the toe rags I arrested off the streets and giving the public a rest, and I'm proud of that,' said Mike.

'Yeah, sometimes I felt I was getting through to people, but others didn't want to know,' said Paul.

'Yes, but the challenge is to reach those people, isn't it?' replied John.

'Did you really believe that?' responded Mike.

'Yes, it was worth the effort but I knew the impact would only ever be partial.'

They walked on past a rocky outcrop and on to another full open, long, sandy beach.

'This really is heaven, isn't it boys?' posed Mike.

'Did you say you had daughters at university, Mike? You didn't mention Mum, is she still on the scene?' asked John.

'Yes, but we are divorced. Early retirement caused some adjustments to my financial arrangements and further negotiations with my ex wife about support for the offspring. They will have to make their own way in the world, as I did, and their mother will have to pay more, which won't cause me to lose any sleep. She did very well out of the divorce settlement.'

'What about you John, what brought you to retirement?'

'Over the years the constant change, erosion of professional autonomy and a hardening of political and public attitudes made the job increasingly difficult….and less enjoyable Mike.'

'Yes, I can relate to that, too,' responded Mike.

'Risk and risk assessment become the mantras, with unrealistic expectations of the power to predict and prevent anything going wrong. I always tried to largely ignore the politics and get on with the job but I was finding that increasingly hard. I wanted to move out to Cyprus, having always enjoyed it as holiday destination. I'm not hung up about being in a multi-cultural and international place, people are people after all and classifications aimed at division aren't helpful. I like the diversity.'

They stopped for lunch at a different beach bar, enjoying the freedom and variety of choice. The range of fresh food on offer in such a modest venue was quite incredible. They each ordered a different choice and beer all round. With the sun shining, the sea gently rolling in, good food and good company, things were definitely looking up.

Chapter 2

Private Steve Mantel settled into his seat on the flight to Cyprus. He had completed his tour in Afghanistan with his unit of the Parachute Regiment and was feeling drained and looking forward to a little respite on the island before returning home to the North East. It was too early to make any real sense of the tour, but he was thankful to have come through it, knowing that some of his mates hadn't been so lucky.

Steve had been brought up on a deprived council estate in South Shields. Jobs were short in the North East following the decline in traditional heavy industry and times had been hard. His grandfather had served in the forces during the Second World War and had fought in North Africa. It was there after the war, while waiting for demobilisation that he had met and married Steve's grandmother. She was originally from Syria and had been displaced by the war and had worked for the British forces in combating the Italians and the Germans. After the war they had returned to England and raised a family. Steve remembered different nationalities at school and in the local area, including some from North African decent. He also remembered fondly stories by his grandmother about Syrian history and culture. Over the years this had influenced him and developed his understanding of the world and that freedom was not an automatic part of many people's lives. It was partly that, but also the lack of viable alternatives that led to his interest in joining the Army. He had played rugby and run cross country at school and was inspired by images of bravery and heroism inherent in military culture. He felt drawn by the challenge of the Parachute Regiment, with its distinctive winged cap badge and red beret. When he started to drift into rough company, bunk off school and dabble in petty theft his father had intervened and told him firmly that it was the Army or eventually prison for him, and he choose the Army.

As he flew towards the military base on Cyprus he was unsure how he would handle the adjustment back to England and seeing family and friends again after the intensity of war.

****

Breakfast followed coffee and Paul, Mike, and John set off to fulfil Hash's expectations of a walk. She scampered off with excitement, chasing sticks, sniffing seaweed and running in and out of the shallows as the sea came in. The three men walked and talked, debating capital punishment interjected by reflections of high profile visits, enquires and inspections. A group of soldiers ran past as a squad, enjoying the morning and celebrating their vibrant youth and fitness.

'I used to be able to do that,' Mike commented.

'I never could,' said John.

'I never wanted to,' said Paul. 'Seems a waste of energy to me.' They laughed.

'Thanks guys, it helps just to have mates and to feel able to sound off a bit sometimes.'

'Yes, give it time Paul.'

They sat on a rock and watched and listened to the sound of the sea.

A young woman approached, running smoothly and rhythmically towards them. Hash suddenly ran towards her nearly tripping her over. Paul responded apologetically. 'Hi, I'm sorry about the dog, she gets so enthusiastic sometimes.'

'No problem, so do I.'

'Are you from the base?'

'Yes, I run this route regularly. Captain Chloe Sanderson, pleased to meet you. Better get on,' and she quickly resumed her pace and gracefully moved off into the distance.

****

Private Steve Mantel arrived in Cyprus, landing on Thursday afternoon. He went through the landing, security and initial reception processes feeling jaded.

He turned to his mate Jack Walton, a tough, aggressive little Scouser from Birkenhead and smiled. They had talked about that first beer, the relief, the taste, the future. Soldiers joining the Army in recent years had been made generally well aware of the risks they were taking. The world had moved on from Germany reinforcement, complex exercises but with little realistic prospect of engagement. Soldiers who joined the Army during the last ten years expected operational deployment. Officers may be motivated by causes, high politics and thoughts of glory, but soldiers generally look for excitement and action, fight for their mates and don't think too deeply about the wider picture.

Steve and Jack had gone through initial training, P Company selection and the parachute course together. They learnt to trust each other, to feed off each other's self assurance and confidence. Bonds forged out of adversity in training bode well for operational duties. Posted to the same section, they joined together, fought together, had gone on the piss together and seen people die together.

In their first engagement, when Steve had become exposed in securing a piece of vital ground against the Taliban, it had been Jack who had covered him by sustained and effective fire from his machine gun. Jack carried a heavy and powerful, belt fed machine gun that was capable of providing covering or deadly fire against the enemy. Jack had a feel for the weapon, his drills were good, but he had the additional qualities of aggressively seeking targets, anticipating enemy deployment and an absolute commitment to supporting his mates to his last breath. Steve had previously put his body on the line for his mate when playing rugby together. They had a bond rarely found outside the military.

The official rational for the deployment to Cyprus as respite was to help soldiers adjust, remind them of what they had lost and achieved, how their country regarded the war, how they might feel on return, the risks of alcoholism, depression and the likely impact on family life. For soldiers it was more of a week on the piss and a chance to fight the locals and the tourists and shag anything that moved.

****

Hash jumped in the car at the end of the walk, happy to lie down and rest for a while. The three men had enjoyed their walk and Paul was feeling more resigned and accepting about facing the future without Sandra. Mike needed to return home to skype his daughters Kate and Abbey about their university applications. They both aspired to be lawyers and had interviews at Manchester and Sheffield Universities respectively. John needed to attend to domestic duties and Paul faced returning to loneliness and isolation.

****

Chloe returned to the camp having completed her run, and showered and dressed for dinner in the mess. She enjoyed the formality of mess life and the attention she attracted. George was in the bar as she entered and readily bought her a slimline tonic with ice and lemon. They chatted about the events of the day; highlights of training, the near miss on the ranges, the latest complaint from the town and the arrival of the 1st Battalion the Parachute Regiment back from Afghanistan.

Captain Chloe Sanderson was the Royal Signals officer at that Army camp. She was tall, athletic & blonde. She also happened to be very bright, ambitious and able. A strong combination of attributes destined to propel her career forward in the modern armed services.

Chloe regularly ran on the beach. This was common amongst military personnel, but unusually Chloe chose to exercise alone. She often ran well beyond the camp to a secluded bay where she could reflect in private away from the pressures of work and constant attentions of the male officers and soldiers alike. This also gave her the opportunity to top up her all over tan. She confidently believed that she was in private sunbathing naked on the beach. The troops knew otherwise. It was worth the 10 mile cross country approach march to keep in training, with the prospect of a better use of Army optical equipment than observing the Taliban, in providing close observation reconnaissance of Chloe's fine form.

Unusually the soldiers were discrete, not wishing to spoil the pleasant distraction from the rigours of military life, or to embarrass Chloe in public, she was an officer after all. Post Afghanistan short deployments to Cyprus were in any event meant to ease the transition back to Blighty and help the men's adjustment and mental health. Whilst not exactly official doctrine most soldiers agreed that this approach helped significantly in that regard.

The British Army has a long association with Cyprus. More recently acting under UN authority it has provided some peace keeping presence since the Turkish intervention and the segregation of the island. Allied military presence could rightly be said to provide reassurance to the local population, contribute to the local economy and add to the culture and diversity of the island. Others would argue however that British soldiers' behaviour is often unwelcome and adds to the unwanted reputation of popular Mediterranean holiday destinations as little more than licence for drunkenness and debauchery. The more politically astute could interpret such presence as either a necessary NATO foothold in the Mediterranean in a potentially volatile and uncertain world or as an outdated adventure in post colonialism.

Whatever view individuals chose to take John, Paul and Mike became increasingly aware of some of the tensions inherent in this relationship between a foreign Army and the local populous. Conversations in bars, local media reports, messages from back home and indeed contact with the troops themselves all indicated some local unease. The British Army base at Dhekelia had become a bolthole for troops between finishing

30

their tours of Iraq or Afghanistan, before returning home. This had in many ways been a positive development in the long history of the Army having to recognise and deal with the impact of battle on individual soldiers and its consequences for retention of personnel and recruitment. Not to mention recovery from injury, both physical and psychological and the wider impact on families and communities when troops return home. Sadly crime, violence, alcoholism and suicide for example are not uncommon amongst troops returning home from conflict.

Historically the Army had struggled with recognising psychological impact as well as physical injury inherent in war in general. In order to maintain discipline and reinforce a culture of stoic determination, resistance to defeatism and absolute confidence in the ability to succeed and overcome, it is difficult to look sympathetically on those who find their response to the rigours of warfare don't quite meet these high ideals. How many soldiers 'shot at dawn' for example, in the First World War were not simply cowards, but those traumatised by their experiences? This dilemma and dichotomy has continued to be a feature of more modern conflicts in for example, Northern Ireland, The Falklands, Bosnia, Iraq and currently Afghanistan.

Developments in understanding the potentially devastating impact of conflict have been as diverse as concerns about 'Gulf War Syndrome', recognition and treatment of Post Traumatic Stress

Disorder and the growth in support networks like combat stress where soldiers can support each other from a position of understanding. The Prison Service has had to develop approaches to dealing with ex military personnel who have fallen foul of the law, with courses being run specifically to meet to unique needs of this group of 'offenders'. All of which is an interesting subject for debate, but for local people the impact can be much more graphic. Pub, club and restaurant owners regularly complained about groups of drunken squaddies shouting, fighting upsetting the locals and other tourists and of course causing damage and nuisance with the inevitable consequences of over indulgence. The Army does its best to smooth local relations but tolerance will only go so far when local businesses face the consequences of such behaviour on a regular basis. Drunkenness and diffusion of tension is however one thing but more serious incidents tend to stay in the public mind for longer. A previous incident of rape of a Cypriot girl by British soldiers caused tensions, embarrassment and strained relations for many years after the event.

As the Army Liaison Officer, Major George Cunningham of The Rifles was used to dealing with such affairs. As a veteran himself of recent conflicts including operations in Afghanistan he knew from personal experience of the costs of war on himself, his family, comrades and the soldiers under his command. He understood the need for a breathing space for troops to unwind and adjust from operational theatres before returning home and welcomed the more proactive stance the Army had adopted. However at times he did admit to feelings of trying to defend the indefensible when faced with upset local people suffering the consequences of 'unwinding' that had gone too far.

The situation across the Middle East was deteriorating. Political instability, old regimes trying to cling onto power, new political movements trying to establish themselves and the West largely standing by hoping that peace and democracy would emerge. In the meantime thousands of citizens were dying, being displaced or found themselves in desperate need. This inevitably set in train mass movements of refugees. Thousands of people flooded into Turkey from the east and into Europe from the south, across the Mediterranean Sea. Despair and human tragedy was growing. While some saw this as an international duty to help, others including criminal gangs saw it as a business opportunity. Where there was desperation and where pitifully inadequate resources were swamped, there was money to be made in offering the gullible a 'fast track' solution.

Movement of vulnerable people seeking a better life and trying to escape from tyranny had become an easy income stream for criminal gangs and a way of diversifying away from drugs, should the pressure to start legalising and legitimating the business take hold. 'People trafficking' had become easy for those unscrupulous individuals who were prepared to trick and trap others for money. They didn't need to kidnap people; like a fishermen in times of plenty, the fish were jumping into their nets voluntarily. The networks needed expanding, but with economic depression across Europe there were no shortage of men prepared to turn a blind eye to the realities of what they were doing by providing transport across the sea to land in the dark on isolated beaches, delivering boat loads of people into the hands of the gangs for onward movement. This practice was no more morale than the ubiquitous slave trade of the 18th and 19th century. People subject to it were at the mercy of their 'escorts'. Some would be exploited by gang masters in sweat shop working conditions, as effectively modern slaves, others would be forced into domestic service across the 'developed' world and sadly young women could be forced into prostitution. None of which would of course be the dream of liberty they thought they were paying for. For those unfortunate young women forced into prostitution, physical and sexual violence awaited; isolation, forced drug addiction and constant threat and fear of being exposed. Adding insult to injury they could find themselves being blamed for their own misfortune and repatriated, penniless back to the chaos they came from.

In Cyprus Stefan Markou had developed this trade, providing cheap labour to service the struggling tourist industry with no questions asked. Also sex workers to staff the inevitably seedy clubs, escort services and undercover brothels that tend to grow in response to a ready supply of tourists with too much money to spend and soldiers far from home. He had an established group of people working directly for him and with a bribe here and 'persuasion' there managed to stay under the radar and go about his business largely unnoticed. The other side of Stefan Markou however was much more high profile. He was a prominent businessman with good connections amongst the local notables. It also suited him to be involved in politics. He moved between voluntary positions of minor political influence, as it suited his purpose.

****

Thursday afternoon was the time for the monthly scheduled liaison meeting between Major George Cunningham representing the Army and George Constantinou, the local Cypriot Police Commander. They shared information effectively and worked well together in what had become affectionately known as the Double George meeting.

'Morning George,' opened the commander, 'let's get down to business. Apart from the regular drunkenness and antisocial behaviour, my concern this month is the growing number of reports I'm getting about illegal immigrants. Legitimate traders are crying foul and complaining about unfair competition. Local services like health and education are struggling and tensions are mounting between established communities and newcomers.

This tends to be played out in the bars. Add tourists and soldiers to the mix and we may well have a problem. What do you think George?'

'Umm, much of this concerns civil governance and is not directly a matter for the Army, but I do take your point. I'll check with the garrison RSM and the military police to see if they have noticed any increase in incidents recently and get back to you.'

'OK. Terrible mess the Middle East now, isn't it? I bet you guys are worried about being drawn into another conflict that you're not resourced to tackle?'

Major George Cunningham tactfully nodded.

'Anyway, the forthcoming visit; how are the plans going from your perspective?' continued the commander. Major Cunningham as a garrison staff officer had been given the task of organising a high profile visit, to take place shortly. They briefly discussed arrangements for both civil and military involvement, before concluding that their former discussion needed to be kept discrete. These types of concern were best played down in public after all.

****

Anya Jabour worked as a lawyer in the capital. She was born in Syria, educated in England and had fled her country in anticipation of the chaos that was to follow. She was Muslim, slightly built and quietly spoken. She had tried to integrate into

Cypriot society, but admitted to finding the tensions difficult at times. She picked up most of her paying business from the British community and spent most of her time helping the ever growing number of immigrants from the Middle East, usually without payment. Anya had a deep sense of justice, a confidence and a powerful intellect to defend the cause of justice against vested interest and prejudice.

She too was concerned about the growing number of immigrants, complaints and community tensions, but not from the same perspective as the Police Commander. Having defended clients against the authorities on numerous occasions when she felt they had a case to be heard, she was well known to the local police and whilst some officers recognised her legitimate role in the process of justice, to others she was one of the enemy, not to be trusted and best avoided.

****

Steve had settled into his accommodation by Friday morning. The first day was intended to be low key, relatively relaxed and an opportunity for some routine attention to kit and equipment and some 'personal admin' time. After ensuring his kit was in order, handing into stores what was required and enjoying a leisurely brunch, he found time on his hands before formal parade. This would be followed by the opening brief about sunburn, sexually transmitted diseases, the effects of alcohol having endured relative abstinence on operational tour, relations with the locals and arrangements for their short stay in Cyprus; colloquially known as 'the pox talk'.

Chapter 3

Steve decided to go for a run on the open space of the beach as a welcome break from the intensity of operational life in Camp Bastion, with its relative claustrophobia. On asking round he soon gathered a group of like minded mates to join him and they set off in familiar squad form to start to get the war out of their heads. Inevitably some individuals coped better with the impact of war than others, but privately it had its consequences for everyone. Whilst they naturally wanted to see home after their experiences, some soldiers could see the thinking behind the interim arrangements in Cyprus. In any event they were here.

They ran with confidence and freedom enjoying the warmth of the sun, the sound of the sea, and the water gently splashing around their legs as they moved along the water's edge. The collective strength and feelings of comradeship inherent in squad running were familiar to them, but today the added dimensions of bird song, dogs barking and cheerful civilians were not. It felt strange but reassuring.

They stopped periodically.

'Down for ten!'

They all swotted down naturally into the press up position and pumped out ten reps, biting the sea, laughing and taunting each other.

'Long way down, eh smack 'ead?'

'Hey, Bentley's using his belly to bounce back! You fat bastard!'

'Piss off, you skinny rake…'

Up they got and ran on, chatting, jostling and digging each other all the way.

'Who's getting the first shag then? Taffy, can you remember what it's for?

'I fancy a crack at them mountains, boys?'

'Each to their own; I was thinking more of two tits and a…'

'Hey! Look at that surfer, fancy that?'

'It's a bloke mate!'

'Down for ten, and sit ups!'

They responded instantly, into the sea without question, emerging panting and wet, but enjoying feeling full of life.

'Contact! Has anyone seen the enemy?'

They all burst into laughter. The relief, the memories, the pain, the loss, the purpose? Each in their own way starting to try to put their experiences into some context, drawing strength from their mates, starting to leave the war behind.

'No fucking Rag 'eads here Corporal, thank fuck…'

In the distance were three static men with a dog and they identified the fixed point as a reference to sprint to. Paul, John and Mike saw them approach without alarm, considering it a part of their training routine, not specifically directed at them. They did however share their amusement and mild relief that they believed this was in fact the case. A squad of fit young soldiers running towards you after all might alarm some people. On arrival at the static point the soldiers stopped and rested. Steve thought that he had lost two keys from his pocket whilst on the run. They had been there since before the tour and he wasn't even sure if they were now relevant, he thought they were from an old gym locker. Never the less he felt an obligation to at least try to find them. Soldiers should look after their kit. The guys agreed to look out for them on the way back.

'Alright guys? That was some pace!' remarked Mike to the squad.

'Yeah, it's a fine day,' replied one of the soldiers.

'We are out for some exercise too, but not up to your standard anymore.'

Just as they were leaving, Steve turned and said 'Guys if any of you find a pair of keys will you hand them in for me at the camp? Steve Mantel, Parachute Regiment.'

'Sure, of course,' and they were gone.

On return the soldiers showered, changed back into uniform and prepared for their parade and briefing. It took the expected form of a welcome to the camp, an outline of the programme and the obligatory warnings designed to avoid negative consequences. On leaving the hall Steve and Jack bantered with Jock and Geordie. They had some tasks to complete, but then the evening was free.

'What are you two going to do tonight?' asked Jack.

'My mate in the Marines told me the place to go is west of the harbour to the new town where there are some good bars and willing girls.'

'OK,' replied Jack. 'Where was it that the officer said we were on no account to visit?'

'East of the harbour, into the old town.'

Jack looked knowingly at Steve.

'Then that's the place to be, see you losers later!' taunted Steve.

The evening progressed from bar to bar with the customary bravado, drinking games and banter. When they found their first bar it was busy with locals and soldiers alike. The locals could always identify the troops as conditioning ensured uniformity translated into civilian dress; i.e. they were soldiers in civvies. It was early evening and the crowds were just getting warmed up.

'Another pint boys? This local lager is OK!' decreed Geordie as he made his way through the morass of bodies to the bar, eyeing up the girls as he went, planning his next smooth intervention.

'Here we are boys...drink up. Seen that blonde over there? Tasty!'

'Yeah, and see all the guys round here?' cautioned Steve.

'I'll take 'em all on!' boasted Geordie, with beer fuelled bravado.

'Come on, let's try the next place,' suggested Jack.

They wandered through the streets of large groups of loud young people out for a good time; singing, dancing in the street, cat calling and barracking each other in the manner of a ritual. Bars, fast food outlets, restaurants and tourist trinket shops shared the space as the area once again played out their nightly scene.

'This one,' cried Jack, as he lead them into a low ceilinged disco bar with music pumping, girls gyrating and guys drooling. They laughed, enjoying the freedom and the sheer fun of the moment with good mates after a hard tour. The contrast was immeasurable and the Army was good enough to recognise this need for a 'buffer zone'. The locals were happy to take their money and the soldiers were keen to make the best of the opportunity. Officially that meant recuperation, for the boys at this moment it just meant a night on the piss.

Pint followed pint and the conversation deteriorated in equal measure. The crowds started to thin out, separating the hard core party animals from the amateurs. The boys saw themselves very much in the first category, but had to acknowledge that they were out of practice. Maybe it was time for a kebab to settle the stomach. After which they separated as they had originally planned, still bragging about which pair would fare the best. Jock and Geordie headed West as instructed, with Jock confident that he could find the action. Jack and

Steve found their way through the streets eastwards towards the old town. They looked around at an area that had obviously seen better days. It was clearly run down. A local man saw them eagerly looking around and watched them for a while before he approached them and advised them where to go with a knowing smile. They looked at each other with anticipation and entered the building he had pointed out. It was dimly lit and a less than inspiring character stood behind a small counter. Requests were made, negotiations completed and money handed over before Jack proceeded towards room 11 and Steve to room 6. Both young men were excited and full of a sense of anticipation, having been largely bereft of female company for months whilst on active service. Both had egged the other on and bragged about their prowess. Privately both also felt some sense of anxiety.

In eager anticipation Steve approached room 6 and opened the door whilst undoing his trouser belt. He entered the room not finding what he expected to see. There was no soft lighting, the sweet smell of perfume or an alluring woman dressed in lingerie lying on a king sized bed urging his friend towards her with a ready smile. No, the room was small, dark and smelly, with no natural light or ventilation and the debris of chip papers and take away food cartoons lay scattered on the floor. It was disgusting. In the corner curled into a ball on a narrow bed was a young girl, no more that fifteen years old, who was frightened, unkempt and silent. Steve took his hands away from his trouser belt immediately and looked at her aghast through eyes of pity and compassion, not of lust, and she started to cry. He was nineteen years old. This girl could be my sister, this isn't right, I'm not having this, he thought to himself. The building was in a poor state but it had previously been a successful hotel and amongst the remaining fittings was still a fire alarm system. Steve looked around and punched the glass setting off the alarm. He took the girl by the hand and guided her onto his shoulders in a fireman's lift, ran down the stairs and out of the building before the bewildered, uninspiring attendant had reacted to the alarm. By the time the authorities arrived they were long gone. They ran hand in hand. Steve new exactly where he was going, he had no doubts. He had seen an advert on the camp welfare notice board in the families room for a local lawyer with an interest in 'human rights', Anya somebody; she would help. They had passed the office previously that night. He didn't know much about the law or lawyers, but instinct told him this was right.

Rasha Ammar felt strangely calm; she knew nothing of the man whose hand she was holding except that he had taken her away from that place... and the look in his eyes...she had seen more humanity and care in that one glance than she had seen during the whole traumatic journey from home to Cyprus. She felt a bond of trust with this man. She had nothing else. They ran through the largely empty streets, past kebab shops, over spilling bins and rubbish strewn alleys. A man was relieving himself in a doorway and another emptying the contents of his stomach on the pavement. As they approached the harbour, Rasha wondered where they were heading on this surreal journey from hell to the completely unknown. She sensed that her rescuer had a plan. She knew she couldn't ask him, but still felt a reassurance in his hand that persuaded her to carry on running, her destination would be bound to be better than where she'd come from. She hoped. She believed. She trusted.

Steve looked back at her, silently enquiring if she was OK. She nodded. He started to slow down as they reached the office door. Steve stopped, obviously looking to check something. He seemed reassured. He was confident. This is where he had brought her and at that moment, that was all that mattered. That was good enough. They sat on the step. Steve cradled her in his arms and held her until she fell asleep.

As the sun rose, Steve thought it best to head back to camp, he could join the revellers as they returned and be unnoticed. He judged that it was safe enough to leave her now. He had spent his euros but took his last twenty quid and placed it into her jeans pocket with a note to Anya explaining the situation and asking for her help. He gently pecked her on the cheek and left in silence. Not a word had passed between them.

He returned to the camp and slid back to his bunk without attracting attention, as he had hoped, just before reveille. He knew he could deal with the day to come. Sleep deprivation went with the job, he was used to it. At breakfast he saw a very worn looking Jack, who seemed eager to talk to him.

'Steve, Steve, what happened you? I was standing in front of this woman with her hand on my cock and then the fire alarm went off! Some stupid bastard must have set it off accidently, as I saw no fire. I thought, I'll finish what I've paid for and was expecting after so long, to hell with a fire alarm! When I left, the place was chaos; women appearing from all over the place wearing towels and not a lot else, an embarrassed looking business type bloke with his trousers round his ankles and another tosser wearing only a smile. What a joke, I headed of for the kebab shop and back to camp for a couple of hours kip.'

Steve laughed slightly nervously and considered what Jack would make of his story and decided it was best to keep it to himself at this stage.

'Do you ever think of anything else but your cock or your stomach, Jack?' he responded.

'Not very often, no.'

'A normal Friday night then?'

'Yes, suppose so.'

Whilst Steve was a young man who had in many ways been saved by the Army from an almost inevitable drift into crime, unlike some of his mates from home, apart from the wild bravado of life as a paratrooper, he had his serious side. He remembered the efforts his dad had made to keep him out of trouble and the attempts to teach him right from wrong. He also remembered conversations with his grandmother about her experiences in the war. She hadn't said much, but it was obvious that she had seen some of the worst of human nature during her time in war torn North Africa before she met his grandfather. He thought again of the girl last night and considered in a different generation, in different circumstances that too could have been his grandmother's fate. Most of his Army mates didn't spend much time thinking about the bigger picture, but Steve found some comfort in at least thinking they were doing right. Wasn't his tour of duty at least partly about trying to prevent events like last night? The girl was obviously of Middle Eastern decent and he wondered about her story.

Anya arrived at the office early on Saturday morning and found an unexpected parcel waiting for her. As the parcel awoke and unwrapped itself, it was evident it was a young Arab girl. Anya spoke to her a shared tongue and she responded in kind. After stilted introductions they went inside and Anya made a drink. The girl was obviously in a poor state, confused and frightened. Anya tried to reassure her. Rasha started to explain the events of last night, obviously wanting to tell someone and again became tearful. Anya placed her hand on the young girls shoulder in reassurance and conveyed that there was no hurry. She could relax now, she was safe. Rasha searched for a tissue in her pocket but found a twenty pond note wrapped in a folded envelope. Anya noticed her surprise and asked to see it. She unwrapped it in front of her. The note simply read: *Anya, I've found this young girl in a disgusting, filthy brothel. I believe you can help her.*

Anya felt a wave of emotion too as she held the brief note as it evoked a whole lifetime of images, memories, events, hopes and dreams, then handed it and the twenty pounds back to Rasha. She could feel a bond between them. She felt they had some shared heritage and faith. Without words she could sense her struggle, her pain and her aspirations. She agreed, she could help her and she vowed that she would.

The two women became better acquainted as Anya started to tell her story in more detail. She had been brought up in Egypt under the rule of the dictatorship. As a child her political awareness was limited, but she remembered family conversations about the Muslim faith and different views about the possibilities for the future direction of the country. She felt that Anya was a Muslim too and she sensed that she could understand. Her recollection was that her family were moderates, not committed to the extremes of Muslim belief and what her father regarded as dangerous extremism. The years of suppression that had fed the collective will to demand better, not really knowing what better would be had lead to what became known as the 'Arab Spring'. The early and unfamiliar experimentation with what transpired to be an illusion of democracy had lead to mockery of an election placing a Muslim cleric in power and control. He was no democrat either. She remembered the village elders meeting and her father saying that it was false to assume that the election represented a powerful support for a Muslim state, let alone an interpretation of Sharia Law. The people had not voted enthusiastically endorsing a Muslim government, but simply voted against fear of the alternative. The result she remembered her father saying was tyranny replaced with instability and potential for chaos. He was proved to be right. This was no freedom.

When the Army started to regain control Muslims elements were blamed and used to justify a return to a military backed regime and the purges started.

Her family lived in an area dominated by extreme views and it was soon clear that moderates were not welcome and were therefore at risk. Her father she remembered didn't want to flee and opted to stay; he wanted to help build a better future. An honourable, if misguided response to the circumstances.

When the Army came to her town there was fear in the air. There had already been fighting, death and destruction. Anti government supporters were said to be in or around the area. Belief was enough. Proof was not required. Muslim ex-government supporters or non sympathetic families were surely to be searched and questioned. Panic ensued with the expectation that any indication of being less than totally committed and loyal to the new state regime would be more than sufficient justification to conclude that you were opposed to it, and therefore were legitimate enemies of the state.

That was the last time she saw her father, or her brothers. Her mother and her were forced to leave from the surrounding area and headed on a slow and desperate trudge with hundreds of others towards the northern coastal towns. Despite all this, in a sense they were lucky. They had some money, some friends and some influence and were able to make arrangements to board a ship. However when the ship eventually departed, Anya could not find her mother and later wondered if she had only been able to arrange one passage and had sent her onboard alone, at least hoping to secure one better life.

As the ship set out to sea it became apparent that this was to be no cruise. The ship was hopelessly overloaded and all basic amenities were in short supply, with travellers left to barter for everything. Currency soon became exhausted and as time went on scope for further barter declined into a downward spiral of ever greater depravity. Anya tried to hide for as long as she could, not wanting to become embroiled in a deteriorating picture of squalor. She had however come aboard with some food in her pockets and two bottles of water, again thanks to her mother. This sustained her for several days, but then risks had to be taken. She believed that it was the third day on board and things were getting desperate. Her hiding place in a storage cupboard was becoming unsustainable. Around that time she remembered hearing shouts and on peeping out thought they indicated preparations to disembark. She emerged from her hiding place to see a small boat being prepared to launch into the dark, she assumed to dry land. She felt in her jacket lining and found the small some of cash that her mother had given her and decided this was the moment to deploy it to its greatest advantage. She moved towards the boat and after some jostling and prevaricating managed to stuff the money into the hand of the man selecting the candidates for the journey. She stepped nervously into the dark to reach the small boat and sat hoping she had made the right call as the boat set off. There were risks. There were always risks. There was no turning back. She felt terribly alone.

The sea was calm as they rode across the waves with a gentle wind and little sound other than the rumble of the outboard and the subdued sobbing of some of the women. Soon she could make out a coast line and could see that the boat was heading towards the shore at a dark and unlit place. People were crying, mothers held on to their children as the boat approached the shore. There were men already waiting, speaking in low voices and in a foreign tongue. She had no idea where she was, accept that it was ashore and that it was not Egypt.

****

The cocktail reception at the mess started, as you would expect, on time at 19:30 hours. It was Saturday evening. The permanent staff officers were politely and efficiently greeting the official guests. Gin and tonic flowed like a mountain stream from the bar, gaining ice and lemon on its journey to the glass. Attached officers and those in temporary residence passing through the transit camp on route to a variety of challenging destinations also enjoyed the hospitality. Captain Simon Middlestone of the Army Air Corps arrived at 19:35 hours and was instantly and strongly drawn to a tall elegant woman on the opposite side of the room. He stood a while to admire and observe while the mess staff worked their way round the guests to offer him an initial glass of bubbly. She looked stunning in a tight little black dress that hugged her desirable form and neatly emphasised her natural curves. She stood opposite a rather full figured officer who apparently held her attention.

'Can I take your glass, Sir? 'enquired the passing waiter.

'Who's the officer opposite in the black dress?'

'That is Captain Sanderson, Sir, Captain Chloe Sanderson, Royal Signals. A gin and tonic, Sir?'

'Yes thanks. Can you pass her this note?' enquired Captain Middlestone, passing a napkin folded over covering a simple message saying *Do you need rescuing?*

The waiter worked his way across the room politely but firmly offering drinks and taking glasses whilst moving closer to the good captain. She was a popular officer, not just for her good looks, but also for her manner with the troops. Officers wield power, but soldiers expect certain standards if they are to respond without question to orders that could lead them into danger. He discreetly delivered the napkin note and indicated its source. She smiled at the aviator and he moved towards her whilst she excused herself from the attentions of the Major. They met in the centre of the room and moved effortlessly to an alcove to be able to talk more easily.

'Thank you,' she said. 'I needed that, he is an awful boor.'

'You look absolutely gorgeous. Are you posted here permanently?' he enquired.

'Oh dear,' she replied, 'can't you do better than that? Maybe the Major wasn't that bad.'

'I'm sorry, would you prefer me to...'

'Chloe, will you join me for dinner? Sorry, Brent Davidson, have we met?'

'Simon Middlestone...'

'Of course Brent, excuse me...' and she floated away.

Simon shrugged his shoulders and recharged his glass. The room was emptying as the guests moved towards the dining room and those experienced officers diverted quickly to the toilets, knowing military etiquette not to leave the table during dinner. Simon found himself standing next to Major Cunningham in the stalls.

'New here? George Cunningham. The Rifles. I see you have met Chloe already?'

'Yes, Sir,' said Simon, smiling. 'No push over then?'

'The soldiers call her the Ice Maiden.'

'Oh?'

'She has her reasons.'

The two officers took their place at the table and started polite introductions to all those in talking distance. The table was laid in customary fashion with multiple layers of cutlery and glasses together with a good collection of military silverware. The centre piece was a large cup dating back to the origins of British military presence in Cyprus. Simon read the inscription; the cup had been awarded in a shooting competition. The starters arrived.

'So tell me about Chloe,' Simon asked George.

'What do you want to know?'

'Is she with anybody?'

'Chloe? No.'

'Strange?'

'There was someone'

'Ah, and she was hurt?' Looking at the Major's face there was obviously more to it.

'Oh no, was he killed?'

'No, worse than that. Alex, he was a cavalry officer, he was terribly injured. He lost both legs and an arm in a roadside bomb on the last day of his tour of duty. The blast also took his wedding tackle, burnt his torso and badly scarred his face. He was an awful mess. Chloe was devastated. They were due to be married within weeks.' replied George sombrely.

'How awful. Poor girl!'

'Opinion was split; some of the family felt she was duty bound to go through with it and support him, but she felt she couldn't, which only compounded his hurt and sense of rejection. Others admired her for her honesty. Whichever way, it was a tragedy for all concerned.'

'Right, so I understand.'

'I don't suppose you do. I'm afraid it's one of the worst aspects of military life...loosing someone that is.'

'Yes, I've been lucky'

'Let's hope it stays that way.'

Simon looked across at Chloe. She was sitting on the other wing of the table. She was next to the Medical Officer. They looked deep in conversation, possibly sharing their experiences of being women in the Army. Chloe had experienced her share of sexism. Some officers and senior ranks still regarded women in uniform as a decoration. However the line had been crossed, women were here to stay. Although not directly deployed as combat troops, although that was being talked about, women were in front line roles and would inevitably take casualties.

'Do you see a life for yourself outside the Army one day, Chloe?' asked the doctor.

'I haven't really considered it, not after Alex's injury, but yes I suppose so. And you?'

'Yes. I do enjoy the Army, but I don't see it as forever. The clinical experience I've had, particularly in trauma has been professionally challenging and I hope to work in a civilian hospital at some point, possibly in A&E...Oh Chloe, I am sorry, how insensitive of me after you talked about Alex! Trauma is not for my medical benefit, I'm so sorry.'

Chloe had got used to people stumbling over what to say, but still found it difficult to talk openly about Alex to almost anyone.

'It's OK, I know you didn't mean it,' she replied, smiling politely as she turned to the officer on her other side. 'How are things with you Claude?'

On the other side of the table, by now tucking into the roast beef, roast potatoes and seasonal vegetables, Simon said, 'Major, how do you find life in Cyprus as permanent staff, with all the comings and going of a transit camp?'

'Wouldn't suit everybody, but I like it. It's a pleasant climate, certainly beats Sennybridge or Catterick, I like the sea and the job has its challenges and rewards.'

'How are relations with the locals now, soldiers being soldiers is it still tense sometimes?'

'It can be Simon, yes. You see the island profile has changed significantly in recent times. There are more immigrants, far more immigrants; I don't know how they get here in such numbers, mostly from the Middle East and North Africa, refugees I suppose. The authorities here tell me that they keep on top of it, but I don't know.'

'So what's the problem? These poor folk have got to go somewhere.'

'Oh Simon, you sound like a bleeding heart liberal! Don't be naïve they come with nothing, can't speak the language, overstretch local services and there aren't enough jobs for the locals as it is, so somebody then has to keep them. And that's you and me!'

'Yes I suppose so.'

'Yes it is bloody so and you remember it captain!'

Sweet, cheese and the obligatory port followed, port being passed to the left of course.

'John, young Simon here isn't familiar with the recent developments on the island, perhaps you could fill him in at your convenience?' said the Major, turning to his other side to address Captain John McIntyre, the Garrison Intelligence Officer.

'Yes, of course, Sir, do call into the intelligence cell next week Simon, you ought to know, you're helicopters aren't you? There is a concern about population pressures and relations between the soldiers and the locals. We try to keep a pretty relaxed regime here, given the task we perform. Troops finishing operations need a bit of breathing space and that's what we aim to provide. I know the garrison RSM thinks that at some point there will be a serious incident involving one of our soldiers if things continue.'

'Well let's hope he's wrong, we certainly don't need this before the visit next week gentlemen!'

****

Monday morning duly arrived and George Cunningham considered his day.

'Call Captain Sanderson and tell her to report to me now Mason,' he ordered his clerk.

'Yes, Sir.'

'Um, I'm meeting the Police Chief and local officials later about the forthcoming high profile visit, I need Chloe to be aware of this,' he thought aloud. 'Ah Captain Sanderson, two minutes.'

'Sir.' While waiting, Chloe talked politely to Mason. He had been in the Army for along time and was looking forward to his retirement. He told her how he had managed to put a little by whilst in Cyprus and had bought a small property in Dorset, hoping to join his sister there next year. How nice, she thought.

'Chloe, do join me, sit down. Two coffees please Mason'

'Sir.'

'Right, I'll just shut the door. The high profile visit. For your ears only and I mean it, this is confidential, this isn't just a routine high profile visit, its scheduled to be a Royal visit. I know the Brigadier's delighted and he knows what it will mean to the men... and women, so special attention required Captain Sanderson.'

'Yes, Sir. Do we know which Royal, Sir?'

'Yes. Moving on, I have a special meeting latter this morning with the key people to present the garrison visits plan. I want you to be the special attendant to the Royal party. It's a great honour and opportunity for you Chloe. These things can make a difference. I know you are ambitious and we all know you are bright.'

'Thank you, Sir,' she replied, thinking he wants me to be the bloody runner!

Mason brought the coffee in on a silver tray.

'And which Royal did you say it was Sir?' Chloe dared to enquire again.

'I didn't. You don't need to know...not yet anyway. This mustn't get out. Oh, and Chloe another thing. Did you enjoy the dinner by the way? I hope you didn't get too much unwanted attention? Simon seems smitten you know? Anyway, this concern about community relations we were discussing around the table. It mustn't get out of hand. Hush, hush, we need to keep a low profile on this one, you understand?'

'Yes, Sir,' she responded confidently whilst thinking Simon, bloody Simon! He must be joking; I'd rather walk on coals or eat seaweed. Simon!

Chapter 4

It was a usual Monday night in the Lamb and Flag, a British owned, British style pub in the town often frequented by soldiers. The landlord John Wilson, an ex soldier himself had seen it all. The bar was full of soldiers largely from one of the resident battalions, on this occasion from the Royal Regiment of Fusiliers, who proudly wear a distinctive hackle of their beret; a bright red and white feather like adornment. Stories were being exchanged and battalion gossip reviewed when a group of Para's from B Company entered the bar. Looks were exchanged and standard insults traded. Reference was made to drill soldiers and crap hats and 'Isn't this the lot that wear a fucking dead budgie on their hat!' responded to by questioning why anyone would want to jump out of a perfectly serviceable aircraft, when it all kicked off.

Blows were freely exchanged, chairs thrown, tables over turned, glasses smashed, noses broken and lips thickened. In short between them, they broke the place up. Sammy McKay and Josh Baker from B Company were more than capable of creating such mayhem on their own, but on this occasion being aided by elements of the opposition regimental boxing team, it was a right bloody mess.

The aftermath greeted the respective RSM's and George Cunningham the Brigade Chief of Staff, the following morning. What was a minor distraction to one was a major incident to another, with more adverse implications for civil military relations. The Para RSM reminded his counter part that they were soldiers after all and the Major shuddered at the prospect of the Brigadier's reaction. The Brigadier a Coldstream Guardsman himself would not be impressed by the prospect of a line of soldiers on parade on Sunday displaying a variety of colourful bumps and bruises.

On Tuesday morning when the CSM turfed out his company prior to the OCs intervention, the RSM was marching past.

'Morning gentlemen, I see I have some more volunteers for extra duties! Some cuts and bruises, I see, I take it that the other lot were left in a worst state than you?' he enquired to muted nods, the soldiers not quite knowing what was coming next. 'Good, that's alright then! You will of course be required to pay for the damage. Don't worry, I have your names and it will be stopped direct from your pay. Some of you had better pray for a quick recovery before Sunday, there'll be no excuses for limping on my parade or looking like the Elephant Man...unless that is you propose to say to our Royal guests that your injuries were the result of hand to hand fighting in Afghanistan, protecting the realm!'

Chapter 5

On Tuesday afternoon John McIntyre walked out to the air strip with Simon Middlestone having given him a preliminary brief. They flew out over the coast and headed west towards Pathos. Captain McIntyre wanted to check on the military training areas and by air was by far the most efficient. He was satisfied. On returning east along the coast they could see troops running along the beach and civilians walking their dogs. The soldiers looked a little ragged. Must remember to mention that to the RSM, he won't be impressed, he thought. A rather rusty looking ship was out to sea on the far horizon.

'Can you see the small fishing boats John? They make a great picture!'

'Um, certainly more attractive than that wreck on the horizon. Did you enjoy the dinner night Simon?'

'Yes, the beef was particularly good. Ready to head back now? Its getting dark and I need to refuel.'

'OK Pilot. Beautiful scenery. What's that over there past the harbour? Looks like a farm warehouse, but why the convoy of minibuses going to nowhere? Beats me, funny things tourists want these days!'

'Maybe a beach BBQ?'

'Maybe. A bit early isn't it? Anyway let's get back.'

****

Mike was walking along the beach with Hash towards the agreed car park to meet up with John and Paul. He could see a helicopter flying overhead. The sea was calm and fishing boats were going about their business, gently bobbing on the water. A group of troops ran past in fine spirits, stretched over some distance. I wonder if that young soldier found his keys? We never saw them, he thought. Mike arrived at the car park and waited. His mates were late. Hash was less than impressed. Mike started to read the local paper. The usual articles appeared; civic ceremonies, rumours of a forthcoming visit, sports reports and tourism. There weren't many jobs advertised but plenty of adverts for restaurants and bars, all competing for trade.

Paul and John arrived together. 'Sorry we are late Mike; got stuck behind a line of minibuses. How are you?'

'Fine, let's walk and talk. OK Hash? A beer later lads?'

****

Simon landed the helicopter OK and refuelled. Um, that doesn't seem quite right, he thought, I'm not happy with that. It wasn't a good feeling for a helicopter pilot as he knew there were few second chances. If they stopped working they had a tendency to go down! I'd better check it out with the techies, he thought. Captain Adam Latham, an Australian had just taken over command of the REME detachment. I'll go seek his advice, he thought and set off across the airfield waving at Chloe as he went. Captain Sanderson did not respond.

'Adam, problem with the chopper, can you have a look?'

'Sure mate,' he responded in his Aussie drawl. 'Jacko, just come and have a look at this chopper with me. No worries mate, I'll give you a call when it's fixed. Just explain to Jacko what the fuck's wrong.'

Simon returned to the mess for some tea. He reflected about the sighting of the ship with John and about his feelings for Chloe and started to email a message to his parents.

After dinner in his room, he was still waiting to hear about his helicopter when a knock came at his door. It was one of the mess staff.

'Sir, message from Captain Latham. Your chopper's been checked and is ready for a test flight.'

Simon thanked the messenger politely and set off to see Adam.

'OK Simon, she's OK, just a tweak, but better give her a test to make sure you are happy.'

'Thanks, mate, I'll take her up now.'

As soon as Simon was airborne he could feel the difference and was pleased and relieved in equal measure. The helicopter soared through the night air with ease as Simon satisfied himself that it was both safe and fully operational. He enjoyed the freedom of the skies and the feeling of being in control. Ever since he was a child he was fascinated by the concept of flight and still felt a sense of wonder that man could design a craft to conquer the skies. As he revelled in delight he observed the lights below, the sea and the coast line in awe and wonder. As he pulled out over the sea his attention was drawn back into sharper focus at the sight of the old ship they had seen earlier. It was obviously still there. He couldn't make out any detail in the dark. Heading back inland, he noticed the movement of a line of vehicles; on closer inspection, minibuses moving away from the beach past a warehouse. It seemed odd. Was it suspicious he wondered?

On return Simon found John McIntyre in the mess and described his observations to him.

'What do you make of that then John?'

'Come on Simon, in a military context this is basic interpretation of intelligence. What does a rusty old ship, anchored off shore in the Med, followed by observation of what could be a fleet of minibuses leaving the beach at night mean to you? Did they have their lights on by the way?'

'Actually their lights came on as they left the lane and joined the main road. The significance being that they didn't want to be seen or draw attention to themselves?'

'Exactly. This looks suspiciously to me like supporting evidence of local rumours that have been circulating about; effectively people trafficking. That ship could be holding people escaping chaos and being illegally assisted to resettle here. I think we best inform the old man about this in the morning, don't you?'

The two agreed to report to Major Cunningham on Wednesday morning and see what action he may want to take.

'Morning Major,' trumpeted Captain McIntyre, 'can we have a brief word this morning, Sir?'

'Yes, best come in the two of you, this sounds ominous.'

'Sir, Simon and I have some evidence from helicopter observation for you that suggests there maybe something in this concern about illegal immigration.'

'You still banging on about this chaps? It really isn't our concern.'

'No, Sir, but we just thought we ought to bring it to your attention. Do we have a duty to report it to the civil authorities?'

'Oh very well, I could mention it to George I suppose, but I'm sure he's got more than enough to deal with without this. OK, leave it with me. Now then, almost time for the CO's briefing. See you both shortly,' concluded Major Cunningham.

John and Simon didn't feel convinced that the old man would take it any further, but at least they had done their duty by making him aware of it. They left for the CO's briefing.

The CO was delighted to inform the whole battalion that Sunday's high profile visit was to be a Royal visit and what an honour and a privilege it was and how pleased the Brigadier was about it. As the soldiers filed away there was a mixed reaction from delight to frustration at their delayed departure.

'Royal visit eh?' said Jock to Geordie. 'You know what that means...three days of pure bullshit and drill... Sheer joy!'

****

John, Paul and Mike found themselves in a bar drinking coffee mid morning on Wednesday, chatting over the days events and plans. The Sun Strip Bar was quite well appointed and presented as pleasant. Behind the counter a man appeared periodically to instruct the barman. He had a presence about him. As they indulged in people watching, the conversation developed into exploring their respective experiences of the rich tapestry of humanity.

'How do you live with the likes of murderers and rapists?' enquired Mike. 'I only have to catch 'em but you guys end up dealing with them closely for years.'

'I've locked up all sorts. Often the ones you think will cause the most trouble are as quiet as a mouse. Not that that means they aren't pulling the strings behind your back. Prison is a strange world of its own, with its own rules. Staff have notional control, but given the numbers only really rule by consent. It's the prisoners who impose their own rules and pecking order on each other, knowing that if they go too far the system will bite back and always win,' reflected Paul.

'It's an odd reality, prison life,' added John. 'We put together the most difficult damaged and dangerous individuals all in one place, away from mainstream society and expect them to learn the skills to re enter that world, often years later, whilst having been apart from it.'

'Does prison work then guys?' posed Mike.

'Now there's a question!' acknowledged John. 'How long have you got? The truth is, it works for some, but it fails many.'

'That's about right' agreed Paul.

The three laughed, acknowledging that they had agreed on something. Whilst they had been talking, over in the corner of the room a senior police officer was sitting with the imposing business man, seemingly in serious conversation. They appeared to know each other well. Other customers came and went as the three settled their bill and proceeded to walk Hash along the beach.

****

Major Cunningham had tasked Chloe with some research, just in case, trying to stay ahead of the game. She had trawled old camp reports and incident logs to see if there was any pattern that might throw some light on the concerns raised by John and Simon. When she returned to the mess her enthusiasm was evident, having completed her task. She walked into the room in time for lunch. George was waiting for her, but something was wrong, she could see it in his face.

'George, job done; you'd have been proud of me, the camp sleuth!'

'Chloe, it's bad news. I'm terrible sorry, it's Alex. He's died and suicide is suspected.'

Chloe collapsed into one of the wing chairs preferred by the senior officers. Tears appeared in her eyes, although she felt a terrible mixture of emotions including relief. Was it now over? Could she at last start to move on? How could she think of that! She chastised herself. Poor Alex, has he been driven to this? In her honest moments she would not have been surprised. What had he got to live for, as he saw it? And she knew his family would blame her...

'I'm so sorry Chloe; I know how difficult this has all been for you and how strong you've tried to be...' George tried to be empathetic.

'Oh George, how sad, why now, why at all?' She stood up and accepted his fatherly embrace. 'I have some information for you George, about the case,' she snivelled.

'Don't worry, its not important. All the arrangements are in hand. You fly home tonight.'

Chloe hadn't had time to take it all in. She had been so excited about her day's activity and now her world was shattered, again.

****

Steve sat in the NAFFI with a cup of tea on Wednesday afternoon. Two visitors were talking with some of the wives about life in Cyprus, not just history, sun and tourism but also the Middle East and its impact on immigration on Cyprus. There were rumours of abuse of power and illegal involvement in the inordinate growth in 'the unofficial population'.

He listened. Who were the visitors?

They continued talking. Maybe the plight of the girl was widespread? He wondered about that; how she is? Had Anya responded to his plea?

Finishing his tea Steve set off to the gym for this year's sports tournament. It had been decided that the sport for this year's tournament would be volleyball and be based on existing sections, i.e. eight man teams, allowing for six players with two rolling substitutes. It would be fiercely competitive, everyone wanted to win. Steve felt confident in his team, they all knew each other well, as did all the sections, but they had two lads who were six foot four and experienced volleyball players, particularly good at jumping at the net.

****

Mason was in the gym as Steve was leaving after his opening matches. His team had got through to the semi finals, due to be played on Friday. The Intelligence Officer had been talking to him and as he left Steve just heard reference to 'suspicious circumstances'. He watched him leave the building then called Mason over.

'Hey mate, what was that, was it about these rumours?'

'Yes, the Intelligence Officer and the helicopter pilot came to see the Major this morning about something they'd seen that looked suspicious down on the coast.'

Mason relayed what he could remember, which gave Steve some idea of where he was referring to. As he went back to his accommodation to continue preparing his kit for the visit and the parade, he thought about the rumours and the girl and the conversation with Mason. This wasn't right, something had to be done.

Later while polishing kit, he shared his thoughts with Jock and Geordie. Jock thought he too had seen a warehouse down towards a beach. Geordie thought this sounded like fun.

'Let's go and have a look then lads!' he suggested.

The others looked at each other and knew a plan was beginning to form. Recce patrols were normally led by officers and consisted of four men. It seemed sensible to stick with that formula. After calling in a few favours and getting Jack on board the four soldiers were packed with enough equipment to start a small war. They decided to set off after tea, when they would just look like soldiers training, going on a march that would not attract attention leaving the camp. Jock tended to take charge in these situations. He had been a lance corporal once, but was busted back down to private after he called his Platoon Sergeant a fucking wanker in front of his men. In fairness to Jock, on that occasion he was probably right but of course the Army didn't see it that way.

After speed marching out of the barracks the four soldiers headed along the coast towards where they believed the warehouse to be. They moved efficiently at a good pace.

After an hour or so they stopped and had a brew.

'So what was it all about then boys, Afghanistan? Was it worth fighting for, worth dying for?' Posed Steve, as interesting questions.

'I try not to think about it,' replied Jack.

'I don't think about it,' confirmed Geordie, 'it's a job, I enjoy it.'

'But what's going to happen after we left?' queried Steve.

'What do you mean, what's going to happen? Another Battalion of keen young squaddies will come along and shoot more ragheads, that's what's going to happen.' stated Geordie with conviction and certainty.

'Yes but, what about the civilians and the country, will it all turn to rat shit and return to the Taliban after we pull out?'

'Yes, probably,' replied Jock realistically, in his dower Scottish accent.

'Then what's the point?'

'You think too much. Does there have to be a point?' pondered Jack.

Steve began to think he was wasting his time trying to engage these three in conversation above and beyond tits and beer.

'OK, better move,' announced Jock, reasserting command.

'We're doing OK, aren't we Jock? It's a piece of piss this Rupert stuff,' said Geordie, postulating his own particular analysis.

The four moved off. Evening was on its way and dark would soon assist their attempt at self directed covert operations. The outline plan was to make it to the warehouse then identify a potential lay up position to construct an observation post, set up their equipment, listen, observe and wait. The indications they had were that illegal landings were happening on a regular basis, so the chances of seeing one happening they thought were good, particularly as the ship was still reported as being offshore.

After another hour's tabbing they began to see the outline of a warehouse in the distance. Jock paused. 'OK boys, quiet now, we don't want to draw attention to ourselves. We are just squaddies on a training march, but the closer we get, we don't want to be seen. OK?' The others nodded.

It was twilight by now. They all felt somewhat excited on this, their own adventure with little or no perceived risk, certainly compared to where they had just been. They paused. There were no lights, no sound of people and no vehicles in view.

'OK, we are here boys' whispered Jock, as he paused. 'Here's what we are going to do. I want Jack and Geordie to stay here and guard this as the emergency RV. Steve and I will go forward to the hedge junction 200 metres in front by the large tree and find a position to set up the OP once sorted. Got your phones lads? I'll text you to join us, OK?'

All nodded, as the advance party moved forward, slowly, quietly and deliberately. At the hedge junction they stopped and observed carefully, all was still quiet, they perceived they were undetected. To their left a slight area of high ground on the edge of a strip of gorse and straggly woodland offered the potential of a good view of the beach area, the warehouse and the road. That was the place. Carefully Jock and Steve moved into position and set up the OP. After a while Jock texted the others and they moved forward to join them, confirming that all was still quiet to the rear.

They watched. They listened. Jock had suggested a standard approach, with two resting and two alert at any one time, allowing for at least some rest during the night. The soldiers quickly settled into a familiar routine. The equipment they had brought allowed for close observation and photography. They hoped to snap anyone present and later identify them. Jock reflected that this was the sort of operation his dad used to talk about in Northern Ireland in the 1970s and 80s. After several hours of nothing, they were beginning to wonder if they were wasting their time. Eventually Geordie interjected, 'Fuck this, I'm off. Just time to get back for some proper kip before tomorrow.'

'You can't just piss off, Geordie!' the others objected and whilst they were insisting he stayed suddenly there was some activity.

'Shhhh,' said Jock, 'what's that? Out on the horizon, a small boat? Hear the engine noise?'

Sounds of voices came from behind them and people started to move towards the beach. Vehicles fired up and several minibuses drove down to the beach from the warehouse without their lights on. As the small boat emerged into focus the beach became a hive of activity, with men starting to organise a reception. One man was obviously in charge. Steve tried to capture him on camera, while the others, all now awake and alert, watched on.

'Careful!' cried Jock in a raised whisper, we could be in trouble here, those men are heading straight for our position. If they walk close enough they'll be literally on top of us. No way we can avoid detection. Oh shit!'

A quick scramble ensued to gather all the kit for a quick exit if necessary, which was in any event an SOP. Suddenly a shout from the beach drew the men away and they changed direction, almost like a drill movement and potential discovery was avoided.

'Oh...that was close,' exhaled Jock. 'Have we got what we need now? Just wait for them to finish and we can bug out.'

As they all nodded, the small boat got close enough for a small number of miserable, desperate, poor soles to disembark. What a pitiful sight; mostly women, some with children, all bedraggled, wet and bitterly cold. Steve could hardly believe his eyes. He had seen many scenes of human deprivation in his time in Afghanistan, but that was war, this was supposed to be a civilised western country. As the people emerged from the darkness the men on the beach allocated them to small groups and hurried them into the transport. Very quickly the small boat set off back and the minibuses were away, down the narrow lane. This appeared to be a well practiced routine.

Steve felt a further wave of revulsion and emotion run through him. How could people act in this way? He thought again of his grandmother and of the girl and of the impact he had seen on civilians in Afghanistan and Iraq before that. It brought back the vivid memory of that day in Afghanistan when another platoon from his company had come under fire and a fierce fire fight ensued. The Platoon Commander called in mortar and artillery fire to subdue the enemy fighters. The next day he was part of a patrol that went out to check the area. They discovered that the shells had done their job and cleared the position and there were no Taliban fighters present, but that was only part of the discovery. The local civilians were incensed, bringing out bodies of dead civilians, including women and children and pointing to damage and destruction in the village. But something wasn't right. The fear in these people's eyes was more acute and distant than would fit the apparent scenario. Local intelligence later suggested that the Taliban action was a deliberate tactic to discredit the Western forces. They had engineered the fire fight, knowing British tactics and anticipating the artillery response. They had withdrawn in time to force local people at gun point from their homes and into the line of fire, knowing they would be killed or injured. They had deliberately caused the damage to key buildings. They then instructed the village elders to wait for the follow up troops the next day and act as if the military response had been responsible for the chaos. They could then claim Western callous disregard for human life, especially foreign human life and the casual acceptance of 'collateral damage'.

All is fair in love and war, they say? At the sharp end, the realities of war being a breakdown of the normal rules of civilised behaviour, with potentially no limits to cruelty and inhumanity. Steve found this difficult to take. Steve was not the first soldier to struggle with such thoughts and no doubt would not be the last. The aftermath of war could cause as many casualties as the fighting.

'You OK Steve?' Geordie nudged him. 'Time to go.'

The others noticed Steve's distant looks sometimes but didn't know how best to respond. Anyway, this was not the time, they needed to move. As they carefully moved off the position, back into the silence of the night, they all felt a sense of satisfaction at a job well done. They had confirmed their suspicions and secured some evidence. Jock was satisfied with that, Jack was pleased for Steve, and Geordie had enjoyed the evening's camping, despite his earlier outburst. Steve however, while recognising their progress, was slowly simmering.

As the morning light appeared on Thursday they moved back to camp to join other groups coming in from exercise for breakfast as if they had not been out all night. No one noticed.

****

Stefan Markou was in the lead vehicle. He turned to his driver and henchman. 'What were those soldiers doing in the area earlier?' he calmly enquired.

'I don't know Mr Markou. Probably just a coincidence.'

'I expect you to know, that's what I pay you for. In my experience coincidences are unusual. You will have an answer for me tomorrow morning. We may have a problem.'

79

The minibuses dispersed and drove off into the early morning, taking their cargo to their pre arranged work locations. Stefan was pleased with his night's work. It was good for business. It was good for Cyprus.

Chapter 6

As they prepared for further practice for the forthcoming visit, Steve wondered again if that was how the girl had arrived. There was only one way to find out, he was decided, he would go to see Anya and try to satisfy his curiosity. Between end of drill practice and room inspection detailed for later Thursday evening, Steve planned to slip out of camp.

When he arrived at the office and entered the front room a young woman was on reception looking down at some papers. She said in poor and broken English 'Hello, can I helps you?' as she looked up at the well groomed and presented soldier in front of her and a smile of recognition crept across her face. Steve wasn't sure as a small woman wearing traditional Islamic dress appeared from behind a screen.

'Hello, you must be the man who helped Rasha, we knew you would come back, I'm Anya Jabour,' she said, holding out her hand.

'Yes, Steve Mantel.'

'So you have met Rasha; as you can see she looks quite the young woman now she is cleaned up. She's sixteen and is trying to make herself useful and learning a little English. I obviously got your note and have arranged for her safety and for the proper papers to be prepared. She has told me her story in her own tongue and of your actions. I commend you for your integrity and bravery Mr Mantel.'

'I only did what I thought was right, Miss.'

'You acted decisively and courageously and I can sense Rasha's gratitude and trust in you.'

Anya led Steve into a back office and the two shared information about their past and their concerns about perceived illegal immigration. Steve learnt more about Anya's involvement in fighting for the rights of those individuals caught up in this mess, how that made her unpopular in certain quarters and the extent of abuse and human tragedy that she believed was unfolding on the island.

'The number of displaced people across the region is huge Steve, but the authorities here still deny it. The number of people coming into the country and other countries along the Mediterranean is even far greater than any official acknowledgement. These are only people Steve, citizens of the world, does it matter where they come from, their race, religion or colour? No, people are people, it's really that simple and these people need our help,' stated Anya, calmly and clearly with boldness and conviction.

Steve noticed that Rasha had come to sit next to him and had coiled up like a cat and had just placed her head right next to him. He didn't know how to react; he wasn't used to expressions of warmth. Steve also didn't want to believe what he was hearing, feared where it might lead him and wondered why as a private soldier he was allowing himself to get embroiled in all of this. Surely it was unwise.

As he arrived back at camp, he wondered whether he should forget all about it. After all, he was only nineteen and had just come through a very difficult tour and needed some space for himself, let alone considering others. There was however something deep within him that felt that to stand by was not enough. Anya had also helped to inspire him and he remembered the feeling of having Rasha next to him and had seen the look of love and relief in her eyes. He knew he had to finish what he started; for his grandmother's sake, if nothing else, but also for Rasha and all those who came before and after her. After all, wasn't that at least in part what he had been fighting for?

All the necessary kit was laid out on their bunks, the room was spotless, the windows had been cleaned and a pleasant fragrance strategically placed to distract the inspecting NCO. Albeit that the can of deodorant had just been extracted from Taffy's armpit.

'Smells like a tarts pants in here boys!' sang out the CSM.

'Now let's make sure all this kit is fit for the Queen!'

'Is it the Queen, Sir?

'Are you a Queen Jackson, did you say?' he taunted.

'N...no, Sir,' Jackson stuttered quickly as everyone laughed.

Sergeant Major White had a well known sense of humour, he was pretty relaxed as Sergeant Majors go, but the troops respected him and always worked hard for him. Inspections were just one of the rituals of Army life. It was just something else to get through. After a thorough interrogation Sergeant Major White was satisfied with all but a few specific points.

'Listen in! Sunday will be a very important day for all of us, whichever Royal appears. Remember you are all representing the regiment, your families and your fallen comrades. Don't let anyone down.'

As he left he called Steve over. 'Mantel, what were you doing in that lawyer's office today?

'Sir?'

'Don't flannel me son, I've got eyes everywhere. You have no business with those kinds of people, you understand me?'

'Yes, Sir,' Steve replied crisply.

'You alright, Mantel? You had a good tour. You can be proud of yourself. It's about winning son. Terrorists can strike anywhere in your home town or mine, against anybody's family, so we get our retaliation in first, that's how it works, alright? We could be looking at you for a stripe son, think about it; Lance Corporal Mantel 'eh? Looking forward to going home?'

'Sir.'

'What you been doing to attract the eye of Mr White, Steve?' asked Jock.

'Oh, just someone obviously bubbled me after going to see Anya Jabour today.'

'And?'

'Jock, just come outside, out of earshot... I've decided, I'm planning something.' Steve announced quietly.

'Steve, what's got into your head now? Wasn't the recce enough? This is in danger of going too far mate, you need to calm yourself,' said Jock, trying to be the voice of experience, calm and reason.

****

'Your answer?' Stefan demanded of his henchman.

'I have spoken to our man Mason, Mr Markou, and he tells me that four soldiers were in our area on Tuesday evening and that this and other reports have been passed to the Major, but that he is still sitting on it.'

'Um, this probably only buys us time. We do have a problem,' replied Stephan resolutely.

****

George Cunningham had heard from Chloe on Friday morning that she had arrived home safely in the UK and was going to see Alex's family that day. He was pleased to hear it, but knew it was going to be tough for her. Apart from her feelings of loss relating to Alex and of what might have been, Chloe could not help thinking of Adam and how they had only just met but that she had felt a spark.

****

Early Friday morning brought particularly fine weather and the prospect of a good day. Hash thought it was an excellent day for an early canter across the beach and fortunately Paul agreed. The beach was not far from where Paul lived, so he had the advantage of being able to step out of his front door straight into a decent walk. They soon reached the beach, allowing Paul to let Hash off the lead. He immediately ran off with a young red setter who was equally mad and the two ran in and out of the breaking waves, loving the company, the freedom and the exercise. Paul was thinking. We have read local newspaper reports, spoken to local people and heard rumours about illegal immigration, but it is all a bit vague. Clearly the situation in the Middle East is dire and this creates refugees, but to me this seems not to fit. On the one hand some immigration, illegal or otherwise seems inevitable, even welcome, but where do these people go and what active steps are the authorities taking to deal with the numbers? It just doesn't add up somehow? He thought back to his prison days and the foreign nationals he had dealt with, mostly for drug offences, many were victims as well as criminals. The scenario often appeared as a too good to be true, get rich quick scheme that hooked the vulnerable in, followed by coercion and threats either to them or their family once the goodies were delivered unless they 'returned the favour'. That usually took the form of being a drug mule and carrying large amounts of drugs with a high risk of detection. The big dealers could take the losses, as the profits were so high that even a 10 percent success rate was more than acceptable. Offering stooges to get caught also helped keep the police at bay and made them feel better. Paul had some idea of the tragedy, disruption and pain people were likely to be going through on their journey out of chaos. Unfortunately where they were desperate people there were going to be unscrupulous criminals who were ready to take advantage of them for money. He also suspected that to be successful on a significant scale, criminal organisations would need to have 'negotiated' cooperation from a variety of official sources. He was well aware that the people who end up in prison tend to be those at the bottom of the criminal food chain not the top.

Paul's mobile rang. It was Mike. 'Hi Paul, where are you? I called round earlier but you were out.'

'I'm on the beach mate, with Hash, at least I was, not sure where she is now!'

'OK, fancy a coffee later, I'll pick up John on the way?'

'Sounds good. Where?'

'The usual?'

'The usual it is. Say half an hour?'

Paul called back Hash from her game and set off for 'the usual'.

The three men met as planned later and caught up on daily events. Hash was pleased to see them and enjoyed the extra fuss from both Mike and John.

'How are you adapting now Paul, is it getting any easier?' asked John.

'Without Sandra, you mean?'

'Yes.'

'A little.'

'Good, well be patient.'

'Listen to him Mike, I'm not on bloody probation you know!'

They all laughed.

'Hey guys, see that minibus parked over there. It's a registration we've seen before. It seems to be a delivery van, at least by day,' observed Mike.

****

All was set for the conclusion of the volleyball competition, to be held in the gym, with large numbers of supporting soldiers to shout encouragement to their teams and hurl abuse at the opposition. Steve and his team were feeling confident and ready to play. They faced a strong team from Support Company, generally older and more experienced guys, these were seasoned campaigners. Mortar men were strong and steady, recce guys more flamboyant and intuitive and sniper troops just focused, cold, determined winners. In whatever grouping, they made a formidable team. Steve and his mates however were not to be intimidated.

The Platoon Sergeant had organised the teams in the absence of the Platoon Commander. Lieutenant Amir had been sent back to England immediately after the tour to join up with the Marines to train as an instructor for the forthcoming battalion winter commitment in Norway. As he had put it on departure; given his Asian routes and recent experience of fighting in the heat of the Afghan desert, the MOD had judged him ideally prepared to be an arctic warfare instructor in Norway! Steve remembered that some of the lads weren't too impressed about the prospect of an Asian officer, but it had to be said that he had proved to be one of the best they'd had and would be missed, whilst they eagerly awaited the next out turn from the Rupert Factory - a term of endearment for the Royal Military Academy, Sandhurst, where young officers received their initial training.

Volleyball entails moving a football sized ball between the players, allowing three movements of the ball to send it over the net to the opposition in a way that makes it difficult for them to return. Games are won on points based on winning such exchanges. At its best it can be exciting, fast and ferocious and bear little resemblance to its more popular commercial version of beach volleyball, where viewers appreciate the athletic prowess of minimally clad young women stretching and jumping before their eyes.

The contest started well and A Company took the lead, with their two key players playing a significant role in smashing the ball down on the opposition from a great height. As the game progressed however, the experience and guile of the Support Company team and their ability to exploit the inexperienced referee began to tell and they ended as worthy winners. C Company took the second semi final against B Company and the Support Company boys went on to win the day!

The CO was pleased with the results of the volleyball tournament, concluded on Friday morning. The troops had got behind it and responded well, generating fierce competition and a good standard of play. It was also a useful tool to maintain and embed section loyalty away from the grim realities of war. He was after all treading a difficult path. On deployment to Cyprus he had been briefed by the Garrison Brigadier that his battalion were due to stay longer than usual for decompression post Afghanistan. This was to take part in the Royal visit, likely to be by the Prince of Wales and the Duchess of Cornwall, no less, and as a parachute battalion to be ready, if necessary to respond to the deteriorating situation in Syria. Whilst the politicians debated on an international scale, the MOD had to make contingency plans, in case it was decided to go ahead with some form of limited operation in Syria involving British troops. A possible scenario could be establishing safe corridors for refugees, for example. The Brigadier had made it abundantly clear how pleased he was about the Royal visit and how sure he was that the CO would be honoured to make his battalion available to take part, albeit at short notice when the two resident battalions had been preparing for this for much longer. Although the CO was one of the public school system's best and a dedicated career officer, he didn't quite share the Brigadier's enthusiasm for ceremony, let alone the prospect of another open ended deployment straight after Afghanistan, and he knew his troops would be less than impressed if all their plans for a heroes' return home and some well deserved leave all went to rat shit. Nevertheless, he accepted his orders like a good soldier. He had learnt the basic lesson early in his military career that if you are going to give orders you have to learn to take them. Further more for obvious reasons both explanations for this change of plan were highly sensitive and therefore secret. The visit had been portrayed as a 'high profile' visit to give it some focus, but its Royal nature had not been disclosed to the troops and would not be until nearer the time. The particular general sense of fondness for 'Will and Kate' was an added bonus! The Syrian scenario was however entirely secret and only disclosed to a very few senior officers on a 'need to know' basis.

The CO had warned his battalion of the forthcoming visit and justified the extended stay on the grounds of a difficult tour leading to a greater need to deal with personnel and equipment concerns properly and sensitively. He was confident that the troops had bought the message.

However, maintaining morale through this period was likely to be tricky, and post leave if the pre existing schedule went ahead there was joint airborne exercises to prepare for with other NATO troops in the autumn and winter operations and survival training with the Marines in Norway after Christmas. Both would require some changes in organisation and structure and the troops would need to be switched on throughout the period. After that he would having to consider handing over his command at the end of his two year tour as Battalion Commanding Officer, probably to take up some boring staff job in the MOD, wearing a suit and tripping over Brigadiers, Generals and the like. Give me soldiers to command any day he thought!

Anyway, he reminded himself as the rain was lashing down outside, I have to see the RSM this afternoon to confirm arrangements for Sunday's visit and I can tell him the full picture now.

The RSM duly arrived, observing military etiquette and custom with an exemplary salute.

'RSM, come in, sit down, are we ready to go for Sunday?'

'Yes, Sir. The troops have got used to the idea now Sir and there is a general sense of excitement. I'm looking forward to it. Although we wouldn't have chosen the timing and we are not a Guards regiment, there is something special about a whole battalion of troops on parade at one time. We just need the weather to come right now Sir,' confirmed the RSM proudly.

'Absolutely! 'responded the CO, 'and I'm sure we were right to decide to parade in desert combats which with our distinctive red berets will not only give a sense of reality to the occasion but will mark us apart from the resident infantry battalions in more formal No2 dress...All the other associated arrangements are in hand too by now I take it; official guests, the catering, transport, entertainment and so on?'

'Yes, Sir.'

'Excellent! Right, one more thing. I can now tell you, which for obvious reason has been kept under wraps; this Royal visit to be from Prince William and the Duchess of Cornwall!,' announced the CO.

'The icing on the cake, Sir! I had wondered.' replied the RSM with a knowing smile. 'Better step up security then Sir. I'll bolster up the civilian guard and ensure extra patrols around the camp and general vigilance.'

The two men parted with a mutual respect cemented by their recent experiences to attend to their duties in preparation for what after all was due to be a genuine day of celebration.

****

A Company were duty Company and the RSM therefore looked to them first to provide the bulk of the extra security required. No doubt there would be a much bigger garrison/civil authority plan involving detailed search, including the use of sniffer dogs, all along the designated route for the day, weaving between both military and civil events. Local security however was down to each battalion to organise and given the sensitive nature of such a visit, its potential for attracting some form of terrorist response and the importance of maintaining good civilian/army relations wherever possible, this was an important task. The RSM briefed his CSM and roving patrols were mounted without delay and arrangements made to bolster the overnight guard. As Steve's section had in the end come out runners up in the volleyball, they were the natural selection for the overnight guard, there being no prizes for losing in this fiercely competitive environment.

Steve completed his duty without complaint whilst others slept, only catching the odd cat nap. As well as the task in hand recent events preying on his mind had also kept him awake. This short deployment was meant to ease his mind, but in reality it was adding to his sense of anger and resentment at what he could see unfolding before him.

Chapter 7

It was in the early hours of Saturday morning that reports first started to come in that the deteriorating weather had led to windy and difficult conditions at sea and that an old ship was in trouble offshore. By 05:30 hours the duty officer in the police control room had taken the decision to alert to Police Commander George Constantinou.

George woke and quickly dressed responding to the call. By 06:30 the first lifeboat rescue had taken place, taking stricken passengers off the ship and to safety.

Commander Constantinou walked into the control room. 'Morning. Right, brief me,' he ordered the duty officer crisply.

'Sir, we have had various reports expressing concern about the presence and condition of an old ship anchored off the southern shore. She appears to be unregistered and ownership has so far proved difficult to trace, Sir. Given the change in the weather, she was first reported to be in difficulty in the early hours of this morning, Sir, and the first lifeboat rescue has just been completed. So Sir, we have the makings of a major incident.'

'I see. How long have you worked in the control room, Officer?' enquired the commander.

'Twelve months, Sir.'

'Well, here's the problem. If we reacted to every call and every unofficial junk that experienced difficulty we would never do anything else. Experience suggests that these types of incidents don't warrant instigating a full emergency rescue plan. Also, if we rescue people in these circumstances we are stuck with them.'

The duty officer was surprised by this reaction. Although information was sketchy, it did seem likely to him that this was a boat full of refugees, how many they weren't sure of and no doubt neither were the crew, but without significant help it was a humanitarian disaster waiting to happen. However, he was not the commander of police and was conscious of his position. Diplomatically he responded, 'So what do you suggest then, Sir?'

'Tell the lifeboat crew to carry on, alert the various civil authorities and let's get a helicopter recce over there now that its light and get a picture of what we are facing. But let's not go public at this stage. I'll brief the press people,' responded Commander Constantinou.

'Yes, Sir, I'll attend to that now, Sir.' The duty officer scurried away to implement his instructions.

George Constantinou spoke to the press office. 'Morning; it's Commander Constantinou, is Archie in?'

'Yes, Sir, I'll get him for you now, Sir.'

'Archie. It's George. We may have a problem. I don't want negative publicity fuelling more attention on immigration you understand. Another junk has got itself into trouble and we need to be seen to be helping, but I want it low key you understand. Emphasise the civic response, play down the impact and the numbers, OK?'

'OK George, I understand.'

By 07:30 several rescue runs had been completed by the lifeboat crew bringing some fifty people ashore. Police and ambulance crews had provided reception but already resources were stretched. The Commander returned to the control room.

'Sir, the helicopter crew report a medium sized ship in poor condition, it's impossible to estimate the number of passengers on board with any accuracy but we are probably talking hundreds. The lifeboat can bring them off, but we need more help on the ground, Sir; the local resources won't cope. We need some volunteers Sir, to at least comb the beaches to identify any bodies. Do I have your authority to launch radio request for help, Sir?' the duty officer reported.

'I see. Yes, OK, but small numbers, and stress a search as a precaution, we don't want to spread alarm and risk putting the tourists off the beaches.'

'In this weather Sir, the tourists fortunately will be in the cafes, bars and restaurants.'

The duty officer soon implemented his suggestion, but still felt uneasy that his commander didn't seem to have fully grasped the situation.

Paul heard the radio bulletin and was happy to respond, regardless of the weather. He and Hash quickly set off for the designated RV. On arrival he wasn't surprised to see Mike there too. A local coastguard official briefed them, assembled volunteers, put them in small groups and allocated sections of coast to patrol. Instructions were to identify and mark the site of any bodies and ring in reports of any survivors.

Paul and Mike, by now joined by John were allocated a familiar stretch of beach and set off.

'It's good of the probation service to grace us with their presence John!' greeted Paul.

'Yes particularly on a Saturday!' added Mike.

'Why, did you two used to work weekends with your organisations then?' replied John with feigned surprise.

The wind was abating and the skies starting to clear as the three men walked across the beach, diligently patrolling their allotted patch. The ground was familiar and anything unusual would be apparent, they thought. Hash ran up and down with glee, back and forth between the three men, taking any opportunity to chase sticks or roll in sea weed as dogs do. Paul was the first to spot it, what looked like a bag or a sack in the distance. As they got closer they feared it was more than that. Hash sensed it and ran forward. Paul wasn't sure how she would react so ran too. As he reached the body, it was evidently an elderly woman. Hash had been gentle but there was no chance of reviving her, she appeared to have been in the water for some time.

How sad, to escape chaos only to drown in the sea and be washed up anonymously on a beach.

Paul reflected on his experiences of death. He remembered finding a young prisoner dead in his cell on morning unlock once, probably from a drug cocktail or overdose rather than suicide. He could remember the emptiness in his eyes and sense of a wasted life, but at least he could be identified and his family informed, dignities that were to be denied to this poor woman. Mike too had dealt with death on duty; from car accidents to murder scenes and had the difficult task of informing relatives of the loss of a loved one. John's experiences by contrast were purely personal and not professional. Probation officers do not witness directly the impact of serious crime, only deal with its after effects; this was Paul and Mike's territory.

With as much respect as they could muster, the men marked the spot and carried on. They hoped she would be their only find, but feared otherwise.

Back in the control room, by ten o'clock things were fraught. The duty officer had tried to convince the Commander of the need for more assistance and was bordering on insubordination.

'Sir, I really must press upon you the need for more assistance; we can't just have survivors stranded on the beach with no provision, it will only result in more deaths, Sir!'

'So we need more help on the ground to deal with the situation as it is now, you are saying? Where are we going to get from?'

'Isn't it obvious Sir?'

'Yes, I suppose it is. OK then, call the military base. I know the resident battalions are both committed at present, but there is the unit just here from Afghanistan – Parachute Regiment I think, they should be able to respond to a crisis,' replied the Police Commander, acknowledging in his thoughts that allowing the British Army a limited public relations coup was preferable to the civil authorities being seen to stand by and let people die, although he didn't want to publicise the immigration problem he was trying to avoid escalating.

It was just past ten o'clock when the CO had settled comfortably in his favourite chair in the mess with a fresh coffee, as the Adjutant marched in.

'I'm sorry to disturb you, Sir, but I've just taken a call from the civil authorities and they have a potential humanitarian crisis on their hands and need our help and they need it now, Sir.' The Adjutant explained briefly what he knew.

'OK,' said the CO who was calm in a crisis. He had been tested many times and had come through well more often than not. 'What have we got here? An old junk ship carrying refugees in trouble in bad weather, offshore. First reports were in the early hours, with first rescue at 06:30. Some fifty people have been rescued so far and the civil authorities are overstretched. It's now 10:15. Why didn't they contact us earlier? Do we know the size of the ship, the number of passengers and how many are already accounted for including the dead?' said the CO expressing his thoughts aloud.

'None of that is clear Sir'

'Marvellous! I can't just fire off at the hip on this one, I need some direction from Brigade, have they been contacted?'

'Not by me, Sir.'

Right Adjutant; gather an informal O group for me with as many Company Commanders as possible, here as soon as you can. Oh, and I want the RSM in on this one whilst I contact Brigade.'

'Right, Sir,' the Adjutant moved off immediately.

The CO contacted the Brigade Major and explained the situation. The staff officer reasoned that the potential fall out from any disruption to a Royal visit was going to be far greater than dragging his feet over giving guidance to the CO on a local rescue mission. He knew he could not contact the Brigadier immediately and as he was on task with the resident battalions he would not welcome being distracted anyway. Also, he thought, should the MOD have a say in this as there were potential implications? It seemed less likely now that the parachute battalion would be deployed to Syria, but the MOD wouldn't want any disruption to tomorrows visit arrangements...nor would the Brigadier. So he vacillated. He agreed to try to contact the Brigadier and get back to the CO.

The CO gathered his thoughts. OK, so no direction from Brigade, but at least they can't say I didn't ask. Syrian deployment being judged to be less likely was welcome and the chances of finding the right civil servant or minister in London on a Saturday morning in time to be able help, he judged to be nil. So, it's down to me, he considered. Can I spare a few troops to help in this crisis? Of course I can, lives are at stake and that has to be the priority. I can scale down the parade if necessary, but surely we can help today and still perform tomorrow, he concluded.

The Adjutant arrived. 'Sir, I've managed to convene four Company Commanders; Support Company are all on the adventure training package today. The RSM's on his way and I've also brought the Medical Officer, Sir.'

'Good man, well done! Right Gentlemen,' announced the CO as he and the Adjutant entered the briefing room, 'this is the situation. As the Adjutant has no doubt told you, we are tasked to help save lives in an emergency and we need to act immediately.' He explained the situation in more detail and the others tuned in to the requirement instantly as he started issuing outline orders.

'RSM, I want you to make contingency plans for tomorrow in case we are still involved and need to reduce the numbers on parade; we could drop a company if necessary.' The RSM was instigating his instructions before he had finished his sentence.

Within twenty minutes vehicles were rolling towards the coast with men and equipment. The Medical Officer and his team set out with OC A Company first to offer immediate first aid and to start to organise a reception area. Volunteers had been sought from soldiers on a simple availability first basis. Steve had been one of the first to respond. He was fit and very determined, had some first aid experience and was a strong swimmer. He jumped onto the lead 4 ton truck together with the whole of the battalion rugby team, still in their kit, who were called off the pitch just before starting a match. The troops had responded in fine spirit, as you would expect, and were laughing and joking on their way to the relatively unknown. The Parachute Regiment traditionally only recruits the fittest and the best; men who can conduct operations at a fast pace; who can remain switched on and react to fast changing circumstances, who are prepared to take the greatest risks and who share an absolute commitment to succeed, to win, to prevail. Whilst in relative terms this was a minor side show for such seasoned troops, it nevertheless spoke volumes for their professionalism that they responded effectively.

On the beach, the MO and his team were straight into administering minor first aid and helping identify those who were priority for the MO or who needed hospital treatment. Most survivors were battling against the cold and wet, as well as lack of food and generally being run down by their recent experiences. OC A Company had seen the condition of the lifeboat crew and ordered them to rest, substituting his own men. As the first 4 tonners arrived he designated priorities and tasks. Immediately troops were helping those ashore who had swum at least part of the way or who had been washed ashore on an incoming tide, holding on to whatever they could to help keep afloat. Others started to strip off without hesitation to get into the water to help, including Steve and the half backs, one centre and a winger from the rugby team, whilst the pack collectively hauled in the lifeboat and its occupants.

Steve swam out confidently towards people in the water. He got to about 200 metres out and the water was cold and turbulent, but he would not be distracted. He saw a woman some way off in front of him with a child on some form of improvised floatation raft. He doubled his pace and swam towards her. As he did so the child became separated from its mother and was in immediate danger. He switched direction instantly and reached him as he was about to go under. The boy could obviously swim but was not used to such conditions, though knew enough to climb on Steve's back and lock his arms around his neck in a vice like grip. Steve reckoned he could swim with the boy on his back and tow the mother ashore at the same time, and headed off towards her. As he approached her she was waving frantically as if to point the other way towards the shore. Before he could reach her he saw a large wave dislodge her grip from her flimsy platform and her slender body disappear below the surface. He was desperate to save her, but sensibly accepted the reality that she was lost to the sea and he couldn't lose the chance to save the boy. Turning towards the shore he started back, with the current, half swimming half surfing towards safety. The boy clung on as Steve had to draw on his reserves of strength to reach the reception party on the beach.

'Fantastic effort Mantel, well done!' cried his Company Commander as he brought his precious cargo ashore. The small boy kept his grip on Steve as he swung him round and others wrapped green towels round him. He smiled at Steve, his grief for his mother would come later, but for now he was safe.

Elements of B Company arrived with tents and a mobile kitchen and soon had erected shelter and started to prepare hot food and drinks. Chaos was slowly turning into order. The substitute lifeboat crew had performed its task and brought home more desperate people, all who were relieved to have got this far. Sadly one old man had died on the boat, unable to summon any more strength.

By mid afternoon OC A Company gathered from his crew and the civil authorities that the numbers available to rescue were diminishing and that the ship was reaching the end of its fight to stay afloat. It seemed likely that RAF air/sea rescue helicopters would be used to reach the final few survivors, taking them directly off the ship.

Steve overheard the MO tell the Major that one of the survivors spoke a little English and had said that there had been no food aboard the ship for five days and precious little water.

'What the fuck's going on Grant? How could this happen?' he had said.

Steve agreed. Another example of why this illegal practice had to stop.

By 1600 hours military operations on the beach in terms of direct rescue were all but over. Some troops remained to help with the clear up and relatively fit survivors still in the tented area, but most were released to return to camp. As they mounted the 4 tonners the troops were in buoyant mood and satisfied with their efforts. After suitable appreciation and rounds of 'well done', they set off back to camp. In Steve's truck the rugby boys sang their complete repertoire of songs and played an adapted two man tournament in the back of the truck using wet towels as the ball. They shared in their own way a strange set of feelings having left the horror of limited modern war behind them, through involvement in this worthy effort, to looking forward to returning home to loved ones and all that would mean.

Steve also wondered why they had been called into action so late in the day. He pondered on the human tragedy, including the boy who had lost his mother today. He then noticed as they drove away that this was the same place he had been in on Wednesday night; there was the warehouse, which the civil authorities had tried to use as a reception area before the tents arrived. How perverse, that these poor sods had been brought ashore at the very spot that their contemporaries had landed only a few days before only to be taken into what amounted to modern day slavery.

On arrival back at the camp, the CO, Adjutant and RSM were waiting to meet the troops. They were evidently both pleased and proud of their men's efforts today and spoke warmly of their admiration and appreciation.

'I'll ensure there is a hot meal available for all these men,' committed the RSM.

'Thank you RSM,' replied the CO, 'and tuck them up in bed before nine, it's going to be a full day tomorrow.'

'There's a growing list of commendations from today's actions, Sir, I'll leave it on your desk. Oh, and Sir, Brigade did come back to me at 1500 hours sanctioning limited involvement in the rescue, albeit with a long list of caveats!' added the Adjutant.

'Thank you, Adjutant! I'll deal with the commendations tomorrow and tell Brigade that's what we did, if it keeps them happy, silly bastards!' concluded the CO with a smile.

Chapter 8

John and Paul reflected on the days events.

'Sometimes organisations can coordinate effectively then, albeit that this was all very last minute!' remarked Paul.

'Yes, it would seem without the 'benefit' of predetermined plans? A sort of spontaneous planning!' retorted John.

'Refreshingly simplicity often works best in my experience,' added Paul, 'so often the greater the role of government, the greater the fuck up!'

They laughed as Mike joined them.

'Yeah, but sometimes we get it right. Look at the advances in our field in working together, over the years.'

'Yes, we did work better together over the years, didn't we? I mean the three agencies, police, prisons and probation. Look at MAPPA for example. That made a real difference in really getting to grips with some of the most dangerous offenders, and likewise with prolific offenders and volume crime.'

Managing these most difficult of cases, placing the balance quite rightly and firmly on the side of public protection, but also recognising that real change is not ultimately about control but demands genuine engagement with the offender to change. By the late 1990's a mixture of political embarrassment, public disbelief and research evidence had brought together two undeniable conclusions; that it was worth the investment to improve agency coordination and cooperation with both the most risky and the most prolific offenders. The most risky; often on being released from prison, often at the end of the state's discretion to prolong the process any longer present particular challenges. The risk of getting wrong and the potential serious consequences for victims place particular responsibilities of those involved. The most prolific, experience confirms are disproportionately responsible for high volumes of crime and often crimes that cause particular public concern, like house burglary. Therefore to concentrate resources and build structures to ensure cooperation between police, prisons and probation services, together with social services, housing, mental health and addictions provision all made sound practical sense. For the politicians this represented that rare combination of factors that would reasonably appeal to popularism, present as innovative and potentially deliver results whilst saving money. Manner from heaven! Attractive to most politicians of all schools of thought by appealing to their first and absolute priority; their own political survival.

This led to the birth of Multi Agency Public Protection Arrangements in the early 2,000's.

'Do you remember when we more often than not didn't talk to each other and by and large didn't trust each other either? The prevailing attitude was to simply do our respective jobs in glorious isolation!' reflected Mike.

Paul had little direct experience of the process, but added 'I know from the prison side that offenders are shit scared of MAPPA and think it has inordinate powers.'

'Do you think the public understand it John?' asked Mike.

'No. I'm sure they don't, nor appreciate the complexities. Most people don't want to know, they just want reassurance that somebody is doing it...effectively. That means of course that it's fine when all goes well and only comes to public attention when it goes wrong.'

'So how do you live with that, John?'

'Mike, it's the same as your job; sometimes you have to just go that little bit further to make it work, but you know that if it doesn't whatever you've done you will be castigated for it.'

'Yeah, you've right; by the press you mean?' responded Mike.

'Yes, but also by your own side! Our MAPPA coordinator used to say that all you can do is satisfy yourself that you've done all you can and that at least makes it easier to live with. He also said remember it's the offender that commits the crime not the agency, which often gets lost in the media drama.'

'Um, hadn't really thought of it like that. Wise words I'm sure John. Don't you think the public just want them locked up and out of circulation though?' posed Mike.

'Yes, but it can be a sledgehammer to crack a nut and its jolly expensive, so the victim gets clobbered twice; once by the offender and then by the taxman to pay for it!' responded John.

'Yes, prison places can cost over £40,000 per year boys. We used to get loads of them brought back to prison for messing up, what do you call it, breach? added Paul.

'Yes, I used to breach then, then Mike's mates would arrest them and hand them to you Paul!' They all laughed. None of them had worked in the same areas of the country, but that put simply was how it works.

Chapter 9

As the guys were getting ready to go out, an item appeared on the television news that caught Steve's eye. There was a report of the ship rescue, which very briefly mentioned the soldiers involvement, then moved on to interview a prominent local businessman and politician for his assessment, including what he thought about the wider issue of growing concerns about immigration. As the camera turned to the man, Steve instantly recognised him as the man they had seen directing operations on the beach on their recce on Tuesday night! He couldn't believe it! Geordie ran in shouting he'd seen it too. As the two men sat in total disbelief, the report unfolded:

'Mr Stephan Markou will be well known to local viewers for his respected position in public life.' Mr Markou noticeably glowed at the sound of his worthy public recognition and praise. 'Mr Markou, can you comment on today's events?'

'Yes of course, speaking on behalf, I'm sure, of all Cypriots, I would like to publicly acknowledge and honour the exceptional role played by our civil authorities in coordinating and executing this rescue,' Stefan Markou responded pompously.

'Weren't some British troops involved too, Sir?' asked the reporter.

'I believe they played a minor part, yes,' responded Mr Markou flatly.

'And Sir, what would you say in response to local concerns about the impact of growing numbers of refugees potentially landing in Cyprus?'

'I can reassure all citizens that there is no evidence to support such concerns and that the civil authorities, working tirelessly on their behalf have the situation fully under control,' stated Mr Markou with absolute conviction.

'So we do not have a current problem with numbers of illegal immigrants, Sir?'

'No, absolutely not,' replied Mr Markou emphatically. Which actually was almost true, at least from his perspective, but not in the way the reporter intended.

'He's a lying bastard!' responded Geordie, with unusual clarity and insight.

'He's more than that Geordie, he's fucking dangerous!' replied Steve, who as a young man with minimal formal education could sense bullshit when he heard it and didn't like crooked dealers in any context.

By early Saturday evening the three young men joined the ranks of soldiers leaving the camp and heading into town for the night. Jock had decided not to join them, warning Steve that he was getting too wound up about all this and felt he was best out of it. They bunked up with some of the rugby lads who were obviously up for a good time, sharing a large minibus as a taxi. They got out early on the edge of the town to avoid suspicion to cries of 'wimps' and general insults from the others. Replying in kind they stepped out of the bus as if they had discovered some extra special bar in the other direction. They waited until the bus was out of sight then dropped down onto the beach and started jogging away from the town towards where they thought the Sun Strip Bar was located. It was a warm evening and they soon began to sweat as they moved along the sand, silently keeping their thoughts to themselves of girls they'd met and those they hadn't, of home and of Stefan Markou.

After a while they stopped and sat in a bar for a drink. The peace and quiet of the location was not reflected in their thoughts and feelings. Steve was angry, really angry. Jack was thinking of home and resenting the prolonged enforced stay on the island. He was also angry because he knew Steve was upset. Geordie just wanted a good night out, with or without a punch up.

'This girl thing has really got to you Steve, hasn't it?' challenged Jack.

'It's not just the girl, the little boy too and there's something I didn't tell you about the night in the brothel. Steve told them the story of his experience, of finding Rasha in such a state and of escaping with her into the night.

'Oh right, so you didn't give her one then?' responded Geordie in disbelief.

'No, I didn't "give her one", you animal, she was a kid! She could have been my sister!'

'I've seen your sister on Skype, she's alright!'

Even Jack gave Geordie a disapproving stare and tried to dig him in the ribs without Steve noticing.

Steve ignored the provocation. He was locked in his own tunnel of thought, anger and resentment. He also tried to explain a little about his grandmother and how she had influenced his life.

'The only influence my gran had on me was when she used to give me sixpence for doing her garden. She had a big old sweet jar that she collected sixpences in and I used to help myself every time I visited. I found the pen she used to mark the line of the coins on the glass and moved it down every time!' Geordie laughed, feeling proud of himself.

Even Jack wondered if this man had any conscious. Having fought with him, he felt probably not.

'I've heard this bars alright, good crack'

Let's hope so, thought Jack, doubting his own thoughts.

The three soldiers moved off again along the beach, Geordie offering deteriorating puerile banter, Steve becoming ever more focused and Jack trying to keep the peace. Eventually the incongruous group approached a line of building development and followed it until they could see in the middle distance a bar standing on its own, with a large title board- *The Sun Strip Bar*.

Their pace quickened, Steve was determined to find this man and to challenge him. At that moment all his feelings of anger and resentment fuelled by his recent experiences came together to focus, irrationally on this one man. He represented all the things wrong in his life; from being rejected by his father, through the brutality of Army training, the horror of war, losing a mate and seeing him fall next to him, feeling the warmth of his blood as it splashed across his face from the exit wound of a sniper's bullet to all that he had seen here in Cyprus. The girl, the others, the mother, the little boy. Someone had to pay and he'd chosen Stefan Markou.

Steve entered the bar, it was early evening. It was quiet.

'I want to speak to this man,' he demanded of the barman, showing him the photograph they had taken on the recce. 'I believe his name is Stefan Markou.'

'There is no one of that name here,' said the barman through cold, detached eyes.

Steve pondered. What next he thought. Had they been wrong? Was this the wrong place? No, he didn't think so.

Stefan Markou could see the three soldiers through his one way mirror behind the bar. He could hear every word. He ensured his CCTV system was working and recording effectively. A door behind the bar opened and a man appeared.

'Gentlemen!' Stefan Markou welcomed them with lavish praise and insincere generosity. 'Our brave British soldiers! I am honoured to host you in my humble bar......Barman where are your manners? A drink, a drink for these brave boys...on the house. Gentlemen, please sit, be my guests,' and Stefan served them their drinks with impeccable manners and self control, helping to disarm them with false reassurance.

Jack was rather taken aback. Geordie loved it, a man who offered free beer, what could be better, he thought. Steve sat and pondered again. He sipped the beer, looked at the others, then at the photograph, the image wasn't that good. The man seemed so genuine. Was he the right man? Was this the right place? He wondered. The others were more focused on enjoying the beer.

Stefan disappeared behind the scenes and grabbed his mobile phone. 'It's me. We might have trouble, I need you and two of your men; bring your weapon. Enter the bar at the rear quietly and wait for me.' He rang off. He didn't need a reply. He knew his instructions would be acted upon immediately. He spoke to the front of house barman on the internal phone, instructing him to ply the soldiers with as much beer as they would take; on the house.

The beer slid down, with jokes and memories, hopes and fears. Geordie was looking forward to being reunited with his wife and baby daughter he had not seen yet. The conversation temporarily steered away from Steve's obsession. The bar started to fill up with a variety of punters. Drinks and food were readily being served.

John, Paul and Mike had been conducting some research themselves and were ready to call in somewhere for a drink when they spotted a parked minibus.

'Hey guys, see that minibus there' said Mike with a policeman's eye, 'it's the same one we've seen before, it's parked at the Sun Strip Bar. I wonder, is that significant evidence to connect Mr Markou with current activities?'

'Could be,' replied Paul.

'Let's go and have a drink and see if the guy is around, we may have something here,' added John.

The boys had just been served another drink and Steve had brought the conversation back to his concerns and his intension. 'Look guys, if this is the man, then he's guilty and he getting away with it and nobody's doing fuck all to stop him. Are you with me or not?' challenged Steve.

The others didn't share Steve's passion for his plan to confront Mr Markou, but a mixture of loyalty and more beer were proving to be a persuasive brew. Reservations faded and emotions rose compounding a sense of loyalty with a belief in invincibility. Steve got up to find the toilet to release some of the beer. As he walked through the bar, picking his way through the other punters he found the relevant corridor. As he walked along trying to identify the gents he noticed that the corridor walls were decorated with a series of framed photographs. All were depicting the same man; his man, the man they'd seen on the beach and on the television news. No doubt in his mind now this was him. All showed Stefan Markou in a variety of situations as a local dignitary receiving awards and commendations. It made him feel sick.

Mike entered the bar, identified a table and the three friends sat down and waited for some service. It seemed busy, but strangely quite tense.

'Is there an atmosphere in here tonight, or is it me?' asked Paul, who after many years practice of managing tensions in prison could readily smell trouble.

'Yes it does seem tense,' replied Mike.

Steve returned from the toilet inflamed with passion and anger. He returned to the other soldiers and announced 'It's him, no doubt. Come on now, you with me?'

Jack had seen that look in Steve's eye before in training and on operations and he knew this could only end badly, but they had gone too far now to back off. It had to be done, loyalty to a mate. Jack got to his feet. Geordie was up for a fight and quickly joined them. Steve pushed past the barman and through the door at the rear where they had last seen Markou disappear. Stefan was standing in the back room with three other men, they all looked up. Stefan stood in the middle of the room with two other men, one either side of him. His driver, henchman was behind him. The three soldiers approached, coiled, ready, prepared. All made the quick mental assessment that three fit young paratroopers were more than a match for the four men they saw standing before them.

Steve looked the man in the eye. 'We know who you are and what you've been doing.'

Stefan didn't flinch. Jack and Geordie both moved forward to take out the two wingers. With practiced precision they took the two men down, leaving them out of action on the floor. Steve moved towards Stefan but the henchman quickly outflanked him to stand in front of his master to protect him. He was holding a knife. Steve responded instantly, moving to disarm the man. The knife crashed to the floor. The three soldiers all looked down and recognised it instantly; it was a British Army issue bayonet. Steve quickly gathered it up but felt a guiding hand firmly grasp his wrist. Stefan skilfully pointed the bayonet towards his failed henchman and tripped him, pulling Steve over with them both. All five men fell onto the floor, falling over the henchman like a collapsing rugby scrum. Steve felt the bayonet push against the man's chest, pierce his skin, deflect off a rib and sink deep into his chest. He could see in the man's eyes the life draining away from him as his chest wound started to make a familiar sucking noise. Instinctively the three soldiers knew it was time to bug out. They started to get up quickly and Geordie headed back through the bar and Steve withdrew the bayonet from the man's chest and together with Jack headed for the rear entrance, leaving Stefan still on the floor. The three convened in the car park and started to run into the back streets instinctively forming up as if in a squad run, knowing that if necessary they could maintain this pace for hours.

Back in the bar it was obvious that something had taken place and people started to look unnerved and to drift away. Mike looked at Paul, 'Wasn't that Steve Mantel, the soldier we talked to on the beach about his keys who just disappeared through that door?'

'Yes, I'm sure it was.'

The two men acted as you would expect to an 'incident', their natural inclination was to intervene, Paul to calm the situation down and Mike to investigate. They looked at each other and proceeded towards the back room. They were met by a terrible mess. Mike wanted to secure the crime scene but they could see that their intervention was unwelcome. They had no authority in this situation and therefore sensibly withdrew to leave this to the legitimate local force. Mike had noticed that Markou was wearing gloves and so was the dead man?

Stefan efficiently went about his business, pleased with his nights work. He had successfully solved two problems. He had dispatched his unreliable henchman, who should have known more about the soldier's interest and had failed to warn him. Failure was unacceptable. He had also ensured that the soldier would be convicted of murder and the other two were insignificant. He quickly dismantled the CCTV camera in the back room and secured it together with the tape in his office safe and removed his gloves and those of his henchman, then prepared to meet the local police to explain how he had been subject to a brutal and unprovoked attack resulting in the murder of a loyal and key member of his staff. He retrieved the CCTV tape from the camera in the bar as evidence to implicate the soldiers. He had always made sure that if his staff were armed they used standard British issue bayonets knowing that if violence had to be used to secure his own interests then he could blame the soldiers. He had already laid the ground with the local press ensuring a constant drip feed of negative publicity, implicating soldiers in violent and drunken incidents. He was calm, he was pleased. He was in control.

'Ditch the bayonet Steve, ditch it! cried Jack as they ran, quickly putting distance between them and the scene.

'Not yet,' replied Steve.

'Those two went down a treat, didn't they Jack?' replied Geordie, as they ran.

'We'll head out towards the beach, so we can run in the sea and clean off any blood,' Steve shouted.

'What happened mate?'

'I'm not sure, after you dropped the first two, but that guy was definitely dead,' replied Steve.

'Come on Steve, we are approaching the beach, you have to ditch that weapon. There, there's a bin behind that take away shop. Bins are collected regularly, no one will ever find it,' ordered Jack.

OK, thought Steve as he wrapped the bayonet in some rag on the floor and buried it in the depth of the stinking bin. They carried on running, onto the beach and into the edge of the sea, washing, cleansing, forgetting.

The local police arrived and surveyed the scene, sympathising with Mr Markou after what must have been a terrible ordeal. They took his statement and the tape, some blood samples and interviewed the barman who confirmed that the soldiers had been drunk and rowdy all night. Treatment was offered to Mr Markou, who bravely declined as the body was taken away and his two wingers were patched up. The scene started to return to normal and the evidence was clear; three drunken British soldiers had brutally attacked a prominent local businessman, killed one of his staff and left two others unconscious. Descriptions were circulated and the officer was confident that they would be apprehended shortly. The British authorities were always keen to be seen to cooperate with the civil powers in such circumstances, in their mutual interests.

Chapter 10

The CO and the RSM met early on Sunday morning as arranged. 'All set then RSM? I'm looking forward to it; I'm sure it will be a good day,' pronounced the CO confidently.

'Yes, Sir, it's not every day we get to meet a future king and his beautiful wife,' he responded.

'Yes, I had noticed,' replied the CO, in chipper form.

'I've checked with all the CSMs, Sir and everything is in place.'

'Excellent!' sang out the CO.

As the two men beamed with pride and expectation the Adjutant appeared looking tense.

'Gentlemen, I'm afraid I bear bad news- its all off! We had a signal at 05:30 this morning announcing that the Royal visit has been cancelled.' The RSM looked dire.

'Surely the MOD haven't cancelled it because of the shipwreck incident?' enquired the CO, in disbelief.

'No, Sir. It's more to do with what I have to tell you next, Sir.'

'Being?'

'There was a murder of a civilian last night in a beach bar and our soldiers are implicated, Sir.'

'Oh,' said the CO, serious, crestfallen and disappointed.

'Stefan Markou, the prominent local businessman and politician was attacked in his restaurant apparently and one of his staff killed and Private Mantel is in the frame, Sir.'

'Mantel? Isn't he well thought of? A soldier with potential?' said the CO. The RSM agreed.

'Wasn't he on the list for commendation after yesterday?'

'He was, Sir, yes,' replied the Adjutant.

'There's going to be diplomatic implications Sir and given the current instabilities the MOD judged the security threat to be too high Sir.'

'Yes, I can see that,' acknowledged the CO, sadly.

'I'll go and stand the men down, Sir,' grimaced the RSM, whilst saluting smartly.

As he turned to go, the CO added 'Hang on RSM, can't we still have a parade and a lunch for the families and invited guests?'

'No Sir', interjected the Adjutant, 'Brigade are dead against it. I'm told the Brigadier wasn't too impressed with your decision to go ahead yesterday Colonel and is hopping mad now apparently and just wants us kept quiet and to be flown out as soon as possible. He's bringing in a Guards Battalion to restore "dignity and calm" as he puts it Sir.'

'OK RSM, thank you. Carry on. We better get Major Cunningham in on this, Adjutant. How long until we fly out? We are pretty well ready. Oh well, the focus changes; its time to pack up and fuck off! The men will be disappointed...all that cleaning and polishing! Never mind, we'll soon get over it! Where is Mantel now, do we know if others were involved?' enquired the CO.

'I understand Major Cunningham is organising all that now, Sir. The QM heard the news and I've never seen drill kit dispatched so quickly as he scuttled off to start organising packing!' The CO smiled. 'Mantel and two others have been arrested apparently on their way back to camp and are currently in the guard room for safe keeping while the civil and military authorities decide what to do next.'

'OK Adjutant, thank you. I'd better go and see Mantel before the RSM gets to him. Whilst he's still alive! Who are the other two?'

'Privates Jack Milne and Geordie Miller, Sir.'

'Miller? Might have guessed it!' retorted the CO, as he left for the guard room.

Collecting the 2IC on the way the CO and his Adjutant walked across to the guard room to see the prisoners. After the customary exchanges with the guard room staff, the CO entered Mantel's cell, who immediately rose to his feet saluting in mid air.

'Mantel, you've really fucked up lad. I'll do my best for you but you realise the system will want to throw the book at you, don't' you? Killing an aid of a prominent local dignitary; causing a diplomatic incident, not to mention disrupting a Royal visit. The type of visit that will only happen here every fifty years and in the circumstances that would have been unique! What on earth did you think you were doing?' demanded the CO.

'It wasn't right. Sir, it just wasn't right.' Steve offered meekly.

'Damned right it wasn't right! What else could it be!' exclaimed the CO.

'No, Sir, I mean what they were doing, Sir.' Steve explained briefly his concerns about people trafficking, Stefan Markou and his actions.

'You can't go simply making wild accusations like that against a prominent member of the Cypriot ruling establishment. Good God man you are only a private soldier!' The CO ranted on for a while until he calmed down. After a pause he looked Private Mantel firmly in the eye and said 'Right Mantel, one chance only, remembering that I may never see you again.... Have you anything else to tell me?'

'What about the Army, Sir?'

'Career over, no doubt about it. Anything else?'

'I didn't do it, Sir, I didn't kill him...Stefan Markou did.'

****

The RSM had stood down the battalion and started to put matters in place to undo arrangements for the day. Official guests had to be informed, entertainment cancelled and the catering manager was frantically trying to off load 600 pieces of fresh salmon to local traders. As he approached the guard room his focus shifted to the three soldiers who were about to experience his wrath. The CO had completed his duty, knowing the RSM's approach would be less subtle, less gentle and more robust.

The RSM entered the room and growled at the guard commander, 'Get those three fucking idiots out here before me NOW!' as the CO, the 2IC and the Adjutant appeared from the rear of the guard room. Even the RSM blushed slightly as he saluted instantly dislodging his immaculate red beret.

'Begging your pardon Sirs, I was just coming to see the prisoners.'

The CO fortunately could see the funny side and winked as he walked past and the RSM smiled. The 2IC and the Adjutant were more po-faced and indignant.

'Take that smirk off your face before I knock it off,' the RSM commanded the regimental policeman. 'You did not hear or see anything. You understand me?' he bellowed, raising his pace stick towards the man's nose. 'If I hear any banter around the camp about this, you'll find yourself charged with murder along with these three fuckers, wherever you were last night! Do you understand!' he demanded rhetorically. 'Now, get me those prisoners!'

The regimental policeman nodded vigorously as he moved down the corridor to unlock the three quivering, soldiers who knew they were about to get the bollocking of a lifetime. They were not disappointed.

Chapter 11

The disappointment of Sunday's stolen celebration had to be quickly replaced by frenzied packing and preparation for departure. Kit polished to death had to be scuffed and scratched while hastily pushed in packing boxes and large bags ready for the flight home. Brigade, the civil authorities, Mr Markou and the press were all responding in their own way to recent events, whilst John, Paul and Mike considered what best to do next.

After it became clear that their attempted response was rebuffed, there was no other sensible option but to return home. By now the three men had a pretty good insight into what each was thinking and shared glances indicated a common view that this was not a night simply to go their separate ways and return to their own single accommodation. Mike suggested his place, being the largest and the others readily agreed to leave the scene and go away for a stiff drink and to consider their options. They were all in an awkward situation; recently retired British criminal justice professionals looking for a quiet retirement, but finding themselves wrapped up in the makings of a murder investigation. Mike had noticed the CCTV camera in the bar and assumed that their presence would have been recorded and that the local police would soon be trying to identify them and seek witness statements. At least that's what he would have done. So, the question was firstly what did they see, what would they tell and should they offer assistance before it being sought?

'What did you make of the incident then Mike?' enquired John, as the three men sat down all armed with a large scotch.

'Well, it looked to me like that guy was dead, or at least seriously injured and whatever happened in there, we did see three soldiers, including we all felt pretty sure, Steve Mantel enter that room just before something happened. So the implication is that there was a fight and the local guy got the worst of it.'

'You mean the soldiers killed him, and a stabbing you thought,' responded Paul.

'Well not necessarily. If it was a stabbing, which did look likely, who knows what actually happened in there and I wouldn't trust that Markou guy as far as I could throw him,' replied Mike.

'Why on the face of it would three soldiers march into a back room in a bar/restaurant and stab a local guy, all in a matter of a few minutes?' questioned John. 'That doesn't sound plausible to me as a spontaneous act. There must have been something else going on to trigger it,' postulated John.

'Um, quite the little criminal profiler now, aren't we?' jibed Paul, and they all laughed, breaking the tension.

'So, what are we going to do guys?' focused Mike.

They had a difficult decision to make. Morally and professionally they felt that they could not just stand by and do nothing, especially as it seemed probable that the local police would be able to identify them and seek to question them anyway. They knew however that once they entered the process there would be no turning back, it was bound to get messy; civil/military relations were sensitive and if Markou was involved in illegal immigration, then vested interests would also be at play. This was not going to be the peaceful retirement that they all had envisaged...at least not for now.

'It's Hobson's choice then guys?' concluded John.

'What do you mean, John?' asked Paul.

'Well, if as it seems we are going to get drawn into this anyway, we might as well jump before we're pushed, so to speak.'

'You mean report to the police ourselves?'

'That might not be wise,' interjected Mike, 'I've dealt with foreign police forces before and you can't assume they operate like ours. My guess is that the investigation will support Markou whatever actually happened, and the soldiers are an easy target and will get the blame. How about we approach the military first? They may at least appreciate our position and welcome a heads up on what happened, as far as we know?'

'And they do speak English!' added Paul.

'Um, could be messy, but a way forward though,' speculated John, 'but if the local police know we've done that, haven't we compromised our position and will no longer to be seen as independent witnesses? Are we trying to help an investigation here, on our own side as it were, or are we simply sticking to a role as witnesses?'

'True, but I don't think we'll be seen as independent and not partisan anyway John,' replied Mike as Paul looked bemused and suggested bacon sandwiches all round.

'We need to agree what's important here,' asserted John. 'There will be all kinds of agendas operating, but for me what it's about is simply a sense of justice and that means seeking the truth...doesn't it?' he challenged the others.

Paul and Mike looked at each other and paused, but they knew John was right.

Tea and bacon sandwiches helped restore some sense of normality before a few hours kip as best they could in Mike's limited space. They woke about ten on Sunday morning and before long the phone rang and Mike answered it.

'Good morning, Sir, is that Mr Mike Tryba? This is Major George Cunningham, I'm the Chief of Staff at the military base. I wondered if I can talk to you?'

'Yes, go on,' replied Mike tentatively.

'I'm rather hoping you might be able to help us. I gather you are a retired police DCI?'

'Yes, that's right.'

'Well, things are a little fraught here at present and whilst this isn't the usual way things are done, I wondered if you might be prepared to come into the garrison to see me, as I understand you and your two friends were present at an incident last night?'

'How do you know that?' Mike responded with a mixture of curiosity and investigative admiration.

'Well it's a small world, Sir, several of the staff have met you locally walking on the beach and I understand you helped out with the ship rescue on Saturday morning? Mason, my man here, who is a mine of information soon came up with a name and contact details. I hope you don't mind?'

Mike looked at the others, who had gathered something of what was being suggested from the conversation and seemed to indicate a nod, so Mike agreed. 'Actually all three of us are here together now.'

'Excellent. I'm afraid there is a sense of urgency, the parachute battalion fly out this afternoon at 1400 hours and I want to make some progress before they go. Can we say 11:00, shall I send a car?' offered Major Cunningham.

'No, that won't be necessary. OK 11:00 at the garrison,' agreed Mike.

'Thank you so much, Sir; I'll meet you at the gate.'

'Sounds like the decision has been made for us.' suggested Paul.

'Yes, overtaken by events. That was quick though, I'm quite impressed. I thought better to hang on to some independence so thought it better not to accept his offer of an official lift,' said Mike as he explained the conversation in full to the others.

Chapter 12

The local police investigator reviewed the evidence from the CCTV footage. It was clear that the three soldiers they had apprehended following initial descriptions were the same three identified in the bar on camera. He also noticed a clear image of three men who might have valuable witness evidence, and tasked an officer to trace them whilst he waited for the results of blood and DNA tests.

Stefan Markou was also interested to identify the three men in the bar, after his barman had pointed out the same conclusion as the police investigator; that they could hold vital information. He was keen to ensure that any such information was registered in support of his version of events and was prepared to offer 'incentives or persuasion' to achieve his desired outcome.

The local press had gone to town on 'the murder of a key local figure' theme. As far as they were concerned the soldiers were clearly guilty and were due to be hanged in public at the earliest opportunity. The military press office had tried to make the best of the rescue story, but it was immediately dwarfed by the media's preference for bad news. As the press officer said to the Chief of Staff 'I'm afraid the reality is, Sir, that you need about nine good news stories to stand any chance of outweighing the impact of one bad. This is about as bad as it gets, it takes us back to the rape incident by British soldiers a few years ago and will put military/civil relations back at least ten years.'

The Brigadier's not going to like that! He thought, and of course it will be my fault, especially now that the Para CO is virtually on the plane. In fact he nearly didn't make it to the plane after the Brigadier had heard the full story and made it quite clear to him that he was not impressed by his impetuous actions on Saturday that could have adversely effected the parade, how could he have prioritised a load of immigrants on a banana boat above a Royal visit, let alone allow one of his soldiers to murder a prominent civilian, for which he held the Colonel personally responsible. The Brigadier had also made it abundantly clear to his Chief of Staff that as far as he was concerned the three soldiers were all to be discharged from the Army immediately and the civil authorities could do what they liked with them, and the more painful and unpleasant that was the better!

The Chief of Staff was basically a reasonable man and his skills in tact and diplomacy had been severely tested in serving the Brigadier who was well known to be a difficult man to work for. On this occasion though, the Brigadier had surpassed himself in his venom against those perceived to be responsible for 'raining on his parade'.

Chapter 13

'Gentlemen, thank you so much for responding to my call,' said Major Cunningham as he met the three 'witnesses' at the garrison gate. 'Do come in and we can talk in private.'

The group went into Brigade HQ and into Major Cunningham's office. 'Mason, some coffee for our guests please.'

'Sir.'

After brief introductions the Major proceeded. 'Right gentlemen, this is the position; civil/military relations are at stake here. The combination of factors in recent events, all of which you are well aware of has caused some major embarrassment with repercussions far beyond these shores. Ministers have been involved, questions have been asked at the highest levels. At the very least it will cost some officers their career and the Brigadier will ensure it's not his. Considerable effort will be deployed to put this behind us and to promote good relations in the future. Sadly it will mean troops activities will have to be severely restrained. We simply can't afford another incident. It is vital that we maintain this base, our foothold in the

Mediterranean and sensible Cypriot politicians acknowledge that, but following that rape case a few years ago, there are the few who have called for the British Army to withdraw. It's that sensitive. So gentlemen...ah, Mason, coffee, thank you...where do you fit in? Well, resources here are stretched my signals officer who would have assisted in this is not available, Chloe...of course you have met her and, how can I put it, my faith in the local police is limited, to bring this matter to a speedy conclusion. Then the perpetrators can get their just deserts through the courts and things can get back to normal, as quickly as possible. I'm sure you agree.' The question was rhetorical. 'So what I'm hoping for from you gentlemen is a clear description of events in the Sun Strip Bar on Saturday night, so we can all get on with it.'

There was a significant pause while John, Paul and Mike tried to take all this in, this wasn't what they expected.

Mike spoke first, 'Major, thank you for your explanation, but I'm sorry to disappoint you but it may not be that simple. Although we were present at the Sun Strip Bar that night we did not actually see the violent incident take place. We can confirm that we believe one of the three soldiers who entered the back room was Steve Mantel, who we had met earlier on the beach, but we can't unequivocally confirm what happened in that room.'

'Yes, I accept that, but gentlemen, we are all experienced men of the world. I know what soldiers are like. Mantel did seem to have got a bee in his bonnet about certain matters, but completely misunderstood the honourable nature of Mr Markou's character, which is beyond question and totally irrationally held some sort of grudge against him. Poor Mr Markou is convinced Mantel intended to kill him and that's good enough for me and I just need your help to ensure the court process gets this one right and Mantel and the other two wasters get sent away for a very long time!' announced George, getting quite carried away.

Again, there was a significant pause, before John tried to gather his thoughts and respond to what sounded very much like a gentlemanly invitation to participate in a kangaroo court...

'I'm sorry Major, but we obviously come at this from a very different perspective. There are due processes to go through here; investigations to be completed and a fair and open trail, none of which are straight forward or quick.'

'Yes, but surely none of that is really necessary when they are all so obviously guilty?' replied the Major, genuinely perplexed at the probation officer's response.

'Major, John's right. We can't just assume that, and there has to be some doubt in this case. What are the soldiers saying about the events of Saturday night?' interjected Mike.

'But you can't take the word of common private soldiers, not in something as important as this!' insisted the Chief of Staff.

'I'm sorry Major, but you must! What have they said?'

'Well,' replied Major Cunningham, beginning to bluster, not used to being challenged like this, 'Mantel has denied it, as he would, wouldn't he? And the other two don't know what the fuck happened!'

'Major,' said Mike assertively, that is for the court to establish, not us.'

'Well, can't you just help a little in an 'informal' investigation of your own, as it were?' suggested Major Cunningham, trying to retrieve something from the situation as it became obvious that his three fellow Englishmen were not as loyal as he had hoped.

'You do realise that would compromise our position as witnesses in the eyes of the court if we do that, don't you?' replied Mike.

'I'm no lawyer, just a soldier, trying to make the best of this mess!'

'OK, I do share your scepticism about the likely depth of the local police investigation, but if I help and the others will have to speak for themselves, it will be in search of the truth, not a convenient version of it from either the military or the civil perspective, is that clear?' offered Mike firmly.

Not used to negotiation and compromise the Major was on unfamiliar ground.

'What do you suggest Mike?' John broke the silence.

'Look, I really can't conduct a full parallel investigation and I certainly can't interview Mantel, that would be completely unethical, but I can go back to the Sun Strip Bar and see what I can glean about what might have actually happened there. How about that?' responded Mike.

After some hesitation and thought the four men agreed in principle to Mike's idea of a way forward. Although risky, it seemed like a reasonable compromise in all the circumstances, and one that they decided that they could live with.

Chapter 14

After a whirlwind few days the CO felt he would rather forget, fearing his career was in tatters, he boarded the plane at 13:45 hours on Monday. As it flew out over the coast leaving Cyprus behind, he couldn't help think – give me command of soldiers any day, but keep me away from politics!

****

Mike drove carefully towards the Sun Strip Bar thinking of what he may find and how best to gather the information. They had worked out their opening moves and after that initiative and intuition were going to have to take over.

'Am I being naive, or was what that guy said simply incredible?' asked John.

'He was pretty brazen wasn't he?' responded Paul.

'Well, we knew it would get messy and right now it isn't going to get any better,' responded Mike in a serious but determined tone.

'The truth, that's all we're after, the truth,' said John quietly and softly.

Mike parked up, noticing that the same minibus was there in the car park again. They walked into the bar, acting normally, talking amongst themselves. As they walked in to the front bar it felt a little odd; quite sad, like intruding too early on somebody else's tragedy, but they had to ignore those feelings and appear relaxed. John approached the barman to express sadness and sympathy for recent events. He felt the man recognised him from the other night as he took their order for coffee. He enquired after Mr Markou and was told that he would pass on his regards but that Mr Markou was not here today. They looked around, nothing had changed in the bar lay out. A German couple they'd not seen before were sitting in the far corner talking loudly and some locals were sitting in one of the alcoves. Paul joined them, having delayed in the car park for a moment. When the coffee arrived Paul commented, 'Did you realise that you had a flat tyre on your minibus? I've just noticed as we parked nearby.'

'No,' replied the barman in a surly fashion. 'You show me,' he indicated and he and Paul left the bar to inspect the vehicle. Quickly Mike walked behind the bar and into the back room, leaving John as look out. It was empty and quiet. He looked around for any indications. There was no blood left on the floor and no obvious signs of a struggle. The room was small, giving little space for seven men to conduct a murder. That suggested to him, as was evident from their own observations that whatever happened must have happened quickly. He looked around the ceiling and something caught his eye; a CCTV mount. It looked functional, but there was no camera present. On closer inspection it appeared that something had been removed, probably in haste as the screw mountings were damaged. Judging by the colour and wear of the bracket whatever was removed had been done so recently.

Paul showed the barman the deflated tyre, discussed the merits of tube verses tubeless tyres, described a selection of his favourite beaches and asked for directions to somewhere he knew well. He couldn't reasonably delay the man any longer and they started walking back towards the bar, with Paul maintaining the conversation as loud as he could. By the time they entered the bar Mike had returned from the back room and was sitting back at the table. As he walked past the barman noticed the three cups of coffee, only the one next to John had been drunk. He expressed his gratitude to Paul for his consideration and said he was confident that he could swop it for the spare later.

The three men casually finished their coffee and said their goodbyes. They walked across the road and onto the beach for a while. 'See anything then?' asked Paul.

'Yes, it seems there is a facility for CCTV in the back room, it looks the same as the ones in the front, except it has no camera in it and it looks to me like it's been recently removed,' replied Mike.

'So you think Markou could have destroyed the evidence afterwards?' posed Paul.

'Possibly, looks that way.'

'Why have a camera in the backroom?'

'Possibly to record the events in case you needed the evidence later?'

'Notice anything else?'

'No, nothing significant, except the size of the room; there wouldn't have been much space with seven blokes in there. Did the barman suspect anything Paul?'

'No, don't think so, but you can never be certain.'

As they returned to the car park, the local police had arrived and approached them.

'Gentlemen, we are investigating a serious incident that took place here on Saturday evening. We have been asking local people if they saw anything, were you here on Saturday evening?'

Mike suspected the question was a test of their honesty and responded 'Yes officer, as it happens we were.'

'Would you be prepared to help us by making a statement at the police station?'

The three men looked at each other and had been expecting this at some point so readily agreed. The officers seemed content to let Mike drive his car, while Paul and John rode in the police vehicle. At the station their attitude hardened, they seemed irritated. They questioned all three men separately and established that they were the men captured on the CCTV footage in the front bar and that they couldn't have seen the fatal incident directly. They didn't seem interested in the fact that they could identify Mantel and didn't ask whether Mike or

Paul had entered the back room afterwards. They did ask them however to confirm that the three soldiers had been drunk and rowdy, which despite their observations to the contrary was taken as a yes. They were then free to go.

'How did they know we were there?' asked John.

'How do you think?' replied Mike.

****

The barman spoke to Mr Markou on the phone. 'Those three Englishmen were snooping around here today Mr Markou. I rang the police and they took them away for questioning.'

'Good, well done. Perhaps I have under estimated you? You can now become my new driver,' replied Mr Markou.

'Thank you Mr Markou, Sir. I'm honoured. Also Sir, our man Mason tells me that the three men have also seen the Major.'

'Then it is time to act,' said Stephan Markou calmly and confidently.

Chapter 15

It was Tuesday morning and the two men had arranged a special 'Double George meeting', given the circumstances. Both were sombre. Mason met George Constantinou and brought him through to Major Cunningham's office. He knocked. 'Sir, the local Police Commander...and yes, Sir, coffee's on its way.'

'You're a good man Mason. Morning George, good to see you, shame about the circumstances.'

'Yes, indeed. You realise the community are very raw about this one George; I can't blame them... and Stephan Markou is understandably perturbed and he's not a man I wish to upset,' responded the Police Commander.

'I understand entirely. You will get my full cooperation and the Brigadier has already made it abundantly clear that he will make no attempt to plead for clemency for the three wasters and will support any civil action. He wants them drummed out of the Army immediately.'

'I see. That's helpful. I did wonder whether you might want to go for military proceedings on this but that makes it plain. The community want blood.'

'So does the Brigadier!' The coffee arrived.

'What has been the reaction to the cancelled Royal visit, George?'

'Disappointment clearly in some quarters, but frankly once the murder story broke I think people understood that such a visit was no longer appropriate. Apart from security considerations, to have gone ahead would have been insensitive.'

'Yes, I understand. Well, perhaps if we cooperate fully with seeing these three wasters hang as it were, then you can see your way clear to a little influence to minimise the potential bad publicity about the cancelled visit?'

'Yes...I'll see what I can do.'

The two men parted on good terms, both feeling that they had achieved what they wanted from the meeting. Mason did too.

****

After their police interview, the three men reflected on events so far. It seemed pretty clear that the key players had already confirmed Mantel's guilt and possibly the other two as well, without waiting for the investigation to be completed. Mike felt there had to be some doubt from what they had discovered so far. He had managed to glean from the Cypriot police that the body was found without gloves, which suggested that Markou had removed both his and those of his henchman after the incident, before the police arrived. There seemed little doubt about his motivation for so doing. He wondered what happened to the weapon. If it was a stabbing, had the local police conducted a search for a knife? If they found something, it seemed likely that any finger print or DNA evidence would implicate Mantel, or possibly one of the other soldiers?

They wondered how the three boys were coping in custody? Presumably they had been transferred to a local Cypriot jail, where you could imagine their presence would not be welcome. Paul explained his experience of prisoner hierarchies and how, at least in a British context the three soldiers would be likely to get a rough time at the hands of other prisoners and he didn't think it would be any different over here.

'So what next then boys?' asked Paul.

'Maybe we should seek some different take on this,' suggested John. 'Say find out what the local legal position is and what the three guys may get, if as it seems they are already effectively convicted. Isn't there a local lawyer who specialises in this sort of thing, a Muslim woman?'

'Yes, I think you are right, Anya somebody isn't it? Has an office in the old town?' responded Mike. 'Shall we pay her a visit?'

Mike pulled up at Anya Jabour's office. She had agreed to see them. The office was in a rundown part of the town and was small and simply furnished. The young woman who sat on the reception desk obviously had a limited command of English. A slightly build woman appeared in traditional Islamic dress and introduced herself, she had a sense of calm and confidence about her.

'Good afternoon gentlemen, I'm Anya Jabour.' They introduced themselves and sat down to talk.

'I assume we can talk in confidence,' Mike stated.

'Of course,' came the seemingly genuine reply.

Mike explained their connection and involvement in the case. Anya briefly explained her interest in the matter. Their initial impression was of a woman of integrity who they could trust. 'If we can talk candidly, there seems a good deal of vested interest in this case and whatever actually happened that night between the civil and military authorities there seems little doubt that the soldiers are deemed to be guilty.'

'That's right. That's how it works here. A few people hold a lot of power and influence and Mr Markou is one,' she replied.

'We need to be careful here,' said John, 'but just how squeaky clean is he?'

'Very clean, at least in the public perception.'

'And in reality?'

'I'm not so sure.'

'Have you met Steve Mantel by any chance or will you be representing him?' asked Mike.

'Yes, I have and I will, but obviously I can't discuss details of that with you,' Anya explained.

Mike explained some of his observations and doubts that the incident was all it seemed. He got the impression that she shared the same view. As they left Anya remarked, 'Just be careful.'

John bought a local evening paper. Coverage of 'the murder' was vitriolic, but the cancelled Royal visit seemed to be played down. Certainly the implication from the letters page was a clear sense of anger and resentment towards the British Army.

The three agreed that it was time to call it a day and head for home. John decided to walk back to clear his head and Mike dropped Paul off at a convenient road junction on his way home. Paul arrived home first, looking forward to the customary greeting from Hash, who had been left in the ground floor flat for far too long today. He opened the door, but there was no welcome and there was no Hash. The dog was missing. It was getting dark as Paul started to search round. In the garden, to his horror he found half a body of his beloved dog. Her throat had been cut from ear to ear. The other half of her he found in the back of his car, with her entrails spread over the seats. It was clearly done to shock and intimidate and Paul had no doubt who was responsible. He reasoned John would be home first and rang him to warn him, but it was too late. John reported that the local police had left him a message that his car had been stolen, they thought by joy riders, and had been found an hour ago. Apparently it looked like a herd of elephants had just run over it. 'I'd better ring Mike; do you think he'll be back yet John?'

'Yes, any time now,' he said , as Paul's phone rang.

'Paul, it's Mike, my villa has been trashed, everything turned upside down. It's a complete bloody mess! It feels like my life has been ripped apart!' Mike reported angrily.

They three men quickly established that each of them had been targeted at around the same time and were in little doubt about who was behind it; Mr Markou.

'Right, we need to act quickly here. It's obviously a warning,' stated Mike, taking charge. 'We don't know much about this guy, but if he has the capacity to 'disappear' people, we could be in serious trouble; we've obviously rattled his cage and I for one don't want to hang about to find out what he'll do next!'

'So what are our options?' posed John.

'This is not a time to piss about,' suggested Paul, 'I say we go straight to see George and ask for protection. We need to lay low for a while or our retirement plans could be very short lived!'

'You mean ask for a safe house?' queried Mike.

'Yes, whatever provision George can offer, but this is the sort of thing our police would do in the circumstances, isn't it? But obviously we can't ask the local police here, so why not ask the military?'

They agreed and without delay Mike collected Paul and John on the way and they all set off towards the garrison, leaving their shattered lives behind. Should we have started this or just stayed out of it, they all wondered?

George was surprised to hear of their arrival as he received a call from the gate. 'Yes I know them, let them through, I'll meet them now.' George responded.

'Gentlemen, what an unexpected surprise. By the looks on your faces something has happened, can I help? I do apologise but Mason is on other duties today, but I will make some coffee.' They all went through to his office. 'So, how can I help?'

Sombrely Mike described what had happened and their conclusions. George seemed genuinely shocked and sad for them. 'Oh dear, how terrible, that shouldn't happen, not at all, not here...' he mumbled.

Coming straight to the point Paul asked directly 'Major, we wondered if you could offer us protection, at least for a while.'

George considered and paused for a while. '...I can offer something suitable. We have a unit on a small island between here and the Turkish mainland. We use it as a sort of retreat for the most traumatised soldiers returning from Afghanistan. You could stay there for a few days. Everything you would need is already there. Stay here, I'll need to make some arrangements, but listen, if we do this you realise I'm sticking my neck out here and the Brigadier won't need any encouragement to lop it off! No one will know at my end, but I need your absolute reassurance that your end is secure, understood?' The three civilians nodded, feeling that was reasonable and in any event they didn't exactly have much choice.

'You will leave your mobile phones here with me.'

'Yes.'

I'll take them now gentlemen,' said George, placing them in his safe before leaving them to make his arrangements.

George needed to speak to Simon Middlestone discreetly about helicopter transport and to the warden on the island, both of which proved to be straightforward. The warden was used to short notice and not asking any questions, he could be trusted simply to facilitate the visit in privacy. George called Simon, who was sitting quietly in his room in the mess reading a book. It was approaching ten o'clock.

'Simon. I have a job for you. No questions, this is secret, you are not to disclose it to anyone and it will not appear on your flight log, do you understand?'

'Yes Sir,' replied Simon, quite intrigued.

'You are to take three passengers directly to our island retreat, the warden will be expecting you, the usual signals and markers on the landing pad apply.'

'Yes ,Sir. Immediately, Sir?'

'Yes Simon, as soon as you safely can. Remember my instructions and follow them exactly.'

Simon got up from his chair, closed his book and started to put his flying gear back on. He was both puzzled and intrigued but had learnt that sometimes you simply don't ask.

George returned to his office where the three men were waiting. They were grateful for his quick and efficient response, but equally were trying to adjust their minds to the new world and circumstances they found themselves in. None of them had anything more than they were wearing with them, but reasoned that this was not the time to be worrying about your toothbrush. The tension broke when John said 'I never really saw myself as working for MI6, did you?' They all laughed as George returned into the room.

'I'm glad you find it amusing!' he commented.

We're sorry, George,' replied John for them all, 'but this is not what any of us envisaged retirement was going to be like!' George could see their point, but was in serious operational mode by now.

'A helicopter will take you to the island shortly. The pilot has been ordered to do just that and the warden is expecting you. Don't attempt to make conversation until you are safely in your quarters, the journey time is very short. Once there you will be safe, I will be able to contact you, but you won't be able to contact me. I shall visit you after a few days and we will decide what to do next. Is that clear? And do remember I'm taking a risk on this one and it is strictly secret.' George reflected that near to retirement as he was, he could afford to potentially jettison the career advancement he never had, but nevertheless he did not want to antagonise the vengeful Brigadier. He knew he was about to be posted soon and would be replaced by Major Llewellyn Michael, Welsh Guards, at the Brigadier's request.

As the helicopter rose into the air the three men reflected that this somehow lacked the grace and charm of a commercial airline, but as it seemed that they were travelling all inclusive, they couldn't complain. George, feeling some responsibility for their circumstances had even arranged for their properties to be attended to and guarded in their absence. He still couldn't believe that Stefan Markou was behind this, but was at a loss to explain it any other way. Perhaps he had been wrong about Markou? Anyway he would talk to George Constantinou about the investigation and consider his next move.

The helicopter landed quickly after takeoff. As instructed they had flown in silence and disembarked from the aircraft without a passing glance at their ariel taxi driver. The warden, an ex Army Sergeant greeted them without small talk and showed them to their quarters. They felt safe, at least for now. At last they could unwind and relax a little and try to make sense of what had happened.

Paul started to smile. 'It's like house arrest, or like prisoners asking to go to the segregation unit when things get too hot to handle! We are in the bloody seg lads!!'

They laughed, John had worked in prisons and could see the joke, Mike also added, 'Yes it's also like being in police cells for your own protection. Suddenly the tables have turned!'

They looked around the quarters and as George had described, everything they could need for a short stay was there; food, catering facilities, clothes, towels, bedding, toiletries, everything. 'I'm not sure I like the colour of the towels,' remarked Paul sarcastically, again reflecting on the average prisoner's reaction to whatever was provided.

Chapter 16

Wednesday morning duly arrived and in the blur of the morning they each looked around and started to piece together yesterdays extraordinary events. Paul rose first, still chuckling to himself about having arrived in 'the seg'. He put the kettle on as Mike and then John started to move and check out the shower facilities. The stock of clothing was basic; mainly light, loose tracksuit style, which for the circumstances was just fine. Again he laughed as Paul adopted the role of the clothing store orderly, being careful to stick to type; to be grumpy, unresponsive and to diligently match individuals to sizes as badly as possible. As the three men sat down to breakfast, each looked like the proverbial bag of shit in their new issued prison uniforms.

The silence of 'the seg' and it's privacy and security however were welcome. Each man had his private thoughts. Paul thought of poor Hash and what had happened and knew how much he would miss her and that those beach walks would never be the same. He also thought of Sandra and speculated what she would have made of all this, indeed if she was still alive he doubted very much that he would have been allowed to get embroiled in this mess at all.

Mike thought of his family and about his villa. What had took a life's work to accumulate had seemingly been destroyed in an instant. He wondered if he would ever return. In his career he had dealt with ignorance, cruelty and depravity. He had also met prejudice, bigotry and at times straight forward corruption, but nothing like this. He had done well in the police force. A lad from a working class background with limited educational opportunities or aspirations, he had opted for what at the time was considered to be a solid career. He had known those who had opted to operate on the other side of the law and was always fascinated by criminal justice and tried to hold on to a simple integrity that it was his responsibility to be fair, firm and open minded in dealing with the public and criminals alike. Unlike some of his colleagues, Mike didn't simply typecast people, or see it as his duty to operate a moral crusade or even to make things fit when there were legitimate gaps in evidence. This was a challenge to hold on to those principals.

John wasn't particularly sentimental about his car. It was to him after all just a means of transport. It certainly wasn't a status symbol. The idea however that after a career in criminal justice, during which he had dealt with some seriously dodgy and dangerous people, largely without incident, that someone could just remove your property and smash it in an instant was unnerving. Of course he had dealt with far worse scenarios, but this was different. He was the victim this time and he wasn't used to that.

As the three men started to share their thoughts at the start of their 'indeterminate sentence', it was apparent that although they hadn't known each other long or ever worked together and had all spent careers in different aspects of criminal justice, they were on the same wavelength. Something fundamentally wrong was unfolding here and it challenged their respective senses of justice and their agreed search for the truth.

'Well, I can't find the monopoly or the jigsaws, so I suppose it's time to sort this out,' remarked Paul. The others submitted to the inevitable.

'There is a flipchart here, shall we try to create a chronology and share what we know and what we think? That would lead to identifying unanswered questions and where we go from here? suggested John.

'Bloody hell,' said Paul, I've just woken up to find myself in 'the seg' and now I'm on a fucking away day with a flip chart!' They all laughed.

'OK Paul, but come on, John has a point, we have the time and an opportunity here to consider what we know and try to make some sense of it. John, are you going to be scribe?'

They started to share their knowledge and established some common ground.

- Markou's man had been killed in the Sun Strip Bar last Saturday night.
- Steve Mantel, Jack Milne and Geordie Miller were all present at the time.
- The fatality appeared to have been caused by stabbing, probably by a knife.
- Immigration of refugees, including illegal 'people trafficking' appeared to be a growing problem, but one denied by the civil authorities.
- Markou appeared to be implicated in illegal activity including 'people trafficking'.
- The British Army stand point was to accept the soldier's guilt, almost without question.
- The local police were convinced of the same before concluding a formal investigation.
- The true details of what happened were not apparent, but there had to be some doubt about the soldier's culpability.

Unanswered questions.
- What actually happened resulting in the fatality?
- How far is Markou involved in crime, undue influence and corruption?
- Why are the Army so keen to sacrifice their own men?
- Why are the local police content to conclude an unfinished investigation?
- Is there corruption between Markou and the police and indeed the Army?
- What happened to the weapon?
- Is it safe to assume Anya Jabour is to be trusted?

- What role did Mason play in events?
- Where would it leave us, if we return to the main island?

John stood back to admire his work. 'There we are then. OK Paul, if that's the analysis of this year's performance we now need to move into setting next year's objectives.'

'Fuck off!'

'Let's just go though those questions for a minute,' said Mike, seriously. He speculated aloud. 'If Mantel didn't do it, is he protecting his mates or was it Markou's men who killed him? Given that only Markou and the deceased were wearing gloves prior to the incident and not by the time the local police arrived, does that indicate some preparation and intent? Also remember the camera in the back room was almost certainly removed. Was it effectively a set up? Given all the key players undue enthusiasm for a quick and simple solution implicating Mantel, does that indicate undue cooperation and vested interests between the police, the Army, Markou and indeed the press?...And is Mason all that he seems given that he would be party to some key information and Markou seemed well informed, is he working for the other side and being paid by Markou?'

'Bloody hell! I never liked away days. Time for some coffee, my brain hurts,' remarked Paul.

Laughter again relieved the tension, as they contemplated Mike's thoughts over coffee.

'Protecting his mates is a possibility,' agreed Paul. 'I know a case of two brothers implicated in a murder and I always reckoned whilst on remand the older one worked out that if he coughed for it, he could save his brother. Why both swing for it, as it were? He reasoned that his brother wouldn't be able to handle the sentence, so he took full responsibility.'

'Thinking about the gloves and the camera,' said John, ' the gloves certainly do suggest that Markou was expecting trouble, whether it was a set up or not, and was prepared. Also, that the camera presumably was to record events and use them if it suited him, which suggests it didn't, otherwise why remove it?'

'Yes, Markou wouldn't have had long before the local police arrived, he would have had to react instinctively, so yes, I agree it suggests he knew the camera footage would not have supported his version of events as an unprovoked attack. I wonder if that footage is retrievable. As for corruption, well that certainly looks likely and Mason's role is certainly questionable in my view.'

'I agree' confirmed John.

For the moment there was nowhere else to go with their thoughts and they all needed a break. In the absence of monopoly or jigsaws, Paul did find a pack of cards and the three men enjoyed an afternoon of going through every card game they could ever remember.

****

George Cunningham sat in his office pondering his career. He had joined as a young officer straight from boarding school and had enjoyed his time in the Army. He readily admitted that he was not cut out for senior command and had been relatively content to remain as the Army kindly put it, as a 'passed over Major'. This had meant a series of postings in that rank between staff and training jobs and he had experienced a variety of settings including operational in different parts of the world. He was now beginning to think of life beyond the Army, not entirely prompted by the Brigadier's attitude to want to attach blame to his loyal Chief of Staff for matters largely out of his control, but primarily because it felt like the right time to move on. Retired officers often stayed in the military family with jobs connected directly or indirectly with military life, but George didn't want to follow that path, preferring to try something new. Running a pub used to be popular, but not so much nowadays as so many pubs were closing. He thought he might like to run a small hotel and had made some initial enquires and taken some opportunities to consider the business skills he would need to acquire. George was single; his wife had long since found the rigours of military life and its impact on families too much to bear and had left him when the children were relatively young. He therefore faced an uncertain and potentially lonely future as he contemplated effectively leaving the only family he had really known. He wondered how he would cope, but for now he needed to address the matter in hand; that was to make some progress with negotiations regarding the murder case and then visit the three civilians on the island retreat, without the Brigadier knowing.

He decided to speak again with George Constantinou and was pleased that Mason, his loyal and efficient assistant, could facilitate the call for him.

'George, its George; how are you?'

'OK. Busy; how can I help'

'George, it's about the murder case. Is there any progress at your end? Here the matter has gone up to the MOD for consideration and the soldiers CO is trying hard to champion their cause, though God knows why, as they are all guilty as sin!'

'Yes, George, the investigating officer had conducted a search along the route that he believed the soldiers took after leaving the bar and has found the murder weapon. It's still being tested for fingerprints and DNA, but you won't be surprised to hear that it is a bayonet used by the British Army.'

'Well that's it then, we were right; guilty. The sheer audacity, not only to blemish the fine reputation of the British Army, but to misuse its own equipment in the process!'

'Wasn't all the parachute battalion's kit securely packed up during their time in Cyprus, ready for return to the UK?'

'Yes, I'm sure it was, but soldiers do tend to keep trophies, and after an operational tour it's difficult to control entirely, but this will certainly mean a crackdown on that practice. Anyway, thank you George, I'll tell the Brigadier that, he'll be pleased to have some good news, at least as far as the conviction goes. You can still count on our cooperation. The Army is very firm with dealing with bad apples and we just want to restore our reputation and build good relations with the likes of your good self George.'

Mr Markou was very pleased to hear the good news from Mason who had been listening in on the conversation. Matters were falling into place nicely, he thought. He was a little concerned however that his warning to the Englishmen seemed to have been heard but that they had not been seen since. This was a loose end and Mr Markou didn't like loose ends.

Major Cunningham needed to know the conclusions from the MOD. He rang the relevant contact. It seemed that the CO had lobbied hard for the three soldiers and won some concessions. The political perspective was less harsh that the Brigadier's view and the makings of a deal was emerging. It seemed likely that Britain and Cyprus would agree to civil proceedings in respect of Mantel and anticipated a life sentence which it was agreed could be served in the UK under British jurisdiction. Milne and Miller were likely to be regarded as less culpable and to be charged under military law for assaulting a civilian and bringing the Army into disrepute, anticipating a six month sentence in Colchester Military Prison, with the option to soldier on after completing the sentence. This was deemed to be a reasonable compromise allowing the Cypriot civil authorities to be seen to have instigated judicial process, calm the public mind and leave the door open for the military to rebuild relations. This would in turn secure tenure of the military foothold in the Mediterranean, not that this had really been in question, but there had been some posturing. Once matters had all calmed down there was even the suggestion that a Royal visit could be rearranged, but that was some way off. George listened intently and accepted what he had been told, although he thought the soldiers had done better than they deserved, particularly Milne and Miller. If the CO accepted that his previous actions had antagonised the Brigadier, then there was clearly worse to come!

Later that afternoon Mason interjected, 'Police Commander Constantinou on the line for you, Sir.'

'George?'

'Yes, results from the tests on the knife; Mantel's fingerprint and DNA are clearly present on the handle of the knife and there are no other traces. Unequivocal George! Unequivocal!'

'Thanks for letting me know George.' Major Cunningham was relieved to hear the case was now beyond doubt. A little later so was Stephan Markou.

George decided on that basis it was time to visit the island retreat and planned to do so tomorrow. In the interests of security he had chosen not to contact the island and assumed that the three civilians would suitably occupy themselves until he arrived. He had made that very clear to them.

George walked across to the Air Attachment Unit to stretch his legs and speak to Simon, who readily accommodated his request for a routine check on the retreat tomorrow. Simon was due to be in the air around that time, so could reasonably drop the Major off on the island and return later to collect him.

****

The Police Commander spoke to Stefan Markou on the phone.

'Mr Markou, it's George Constantinou. We need to talk. Things are happening fast, there is no time to meet; can you talk confidentially?'

'All my calls are confidential, Police Commander, and I can always talk to you,' replied Stefan Markou in a sycophantic manner.

The Police Commander relayed the MODs position, which helpfully confirmed Markou's source and that the three Englishmen had not been seen since his intervention. George Constantinou also explained about the bayonet evidence and concluded that the case against the soldiers was now water tight. Stephan Markou agreed and expressed satisfaction with the proposals. It was Mantel that he wanted after all, particularly after he had inconsiderably and despicably rescued that girl who Markou had specifically ordered for his own personal attention. He didn't care about the other two. There was some satisfaction in knowing that the man who had let him down by not sending her directly to him was no longer going to inconvenience him from his new location in a secure box at the bottom of the sea.

'Given what has transpired, I take it that if those Englishmen do reappear and I hope you haven't ensured that they don't, assuming they heed the first message and don't interfere with matters that don't concern them again, then you will leave them alone? I don't want any more incidents.'

Stephan Markou was not aware that the Police Commander knew so much about his tactics and 'arrangements'. 'Yes, Police Commander, I agree, the Englishmen are no longer of any consequence or interest to me.'

Major Cunningham was just preparing to leave when Mason put through another call from the Police Commander.

'Quickly, by the way George, my intelligence sources tell me that whatever happened to the three Englishmen, given the certainty of the case now, Mr Markou is unlikely to present a threat to them. As regards their recent unfortunate experiences, you will understand that I can't associate any of that with Mr Markou. I have already concluded that it was a random response to the uprising of anti English feeling following the murder and closed the file. I assume you had heard about that?'

'OK, yes I had heard some rumour. I accept what you say George, we don't want any more bad publicity for the Island, none of us do. It's for the best. I haven't seen the three Englishmen recently either,' replied the Major, which was at least reasonably true, if you take 'recently' to mean about the last 24 hours!

****

In the retreat the three friends had used their time effectively, not just to rest but to speculate on some of the motivations for recent events. In the circumstances of their confinement it almost felt like some kind of perverse parlour game.

'Politics is a strange business isn't it? I've never had much faith in politicians of any persuasion,' remarked Paul.

'You're not alone there,' added Mike. 'Yes politics is a murky business at best. Who knows what alliances have been forged in the upper echelons of the Cypriot elite with the British Army and the British Government? There are some pretty big strategic issues at stake here.'

'Bloody hell, swallowed a dictionary? You're off now! Time for lunch.' interjected Paul.

'Yes, sorry. Reality check... If the motivation for the big institutional players is clear, that is basically preserving reputation and the status quo, what would be the potential motivation for Markou in this?'

'I've been thinking about that,' responded John.

'Here we go!' anticipated Paul.

John smiled. 'Paul you must have met guys like Markou inside? He strikes me as a potential psychopath.'

'Go on,' said Mike.

'He obviously likes to be in control, he doesn't seem to have any empathy or feeling for anybody else's perspective and he engages in the pursuit of power at any price. That's not a bad match for starters for potential psychopathic traits.'

'Yes, allowing for your tendency to slip into criminal profiler mode, you might have something there. Yes, I've met men like him inside, ruthless, cold, calculating. They simply use people to manipulate events and have no moral compass and operate on the basis of pure self interest.'

'I agree,' Mike added. It's not only the usual criminal who can act like that, mild psychopathic traits can be in successful people more generally. Absolute self belief and determination after all are quite useful qualities to reach the top in most organisations, and sadly being personable doesn't always get you very far.' They all agreed from their own experience.

'So if Markou is psychopathic, so what?' speculated Paul.

'Well I guess that suggests that he is ruthless and will stop at virtually nothing to fulfil his goals, therefore that makes him very dangerous...' concluded John sombrely.

Silence fell between them over lunch as they heard the sound of a helicopter. It was 14:05 hours on Thursday. After a few minutes, although it felt much longer, George appeared in 'the seg'.

'Sorry about the wait,' George announced. 'I had intended to be here earlier, but the weather intervened. I'm sure you have managed to keep entertained? I see you have found the clothing store...um, looks like fancy dress!'

They all chuckled and Paul shared their amusement about perceptions of the segregation unit.

'So, gentlemen, I bring some news. Some good, some bad,' said George seriously.

'OK, let's have the bad news first,' responded Paul, whilst the others were thinking the same.

'OK, well, I've spoken to the local Police Commander and the MOD, and the picture basically is this; the police are convinced of the strength of their case to charge Mantel with murder, and the MOD for diplomatic and political reasons have accepted that and negotiated an agreement for Mantel to serve the anticipated life sentence under British jurisdiction. Given that I am advised that Markou's interest in you will cease, as long that is that you play no further part in local affairs and just get on with your retirement.'

'OK,' responded Mike cautiously, 'and what of the other two?'

'Milne and Miller are expected to be left to military jurisdiction which will mean six months in Colchester and carry on.'

'Oh, not too bad then?' replied Mike.

'Unless you are Steve Mantel,' replied John. 'So, why the sudden change to even greater certainty?'

'I'm sorry. The key development is that the police found the murder weapon; a British Army bayonet. Scientific evidence confirmed Mantel was responsible, so the evidence is unequivocal.'

'Really?' queried Mike, 'That clear cut?'

'Yes, apparently so.'

'What about Markou? Can't the local police stick anything on him? asked Mike.

'No, apparently not. Can't say more old boy, replied George.

After a pause, Paul responded stoutly, 'And you can live with that? One of your soldiers gets a life sentence on what looks like a stitch up and Markou walks away scot free to carry on his corrupt and criminal lifestyle?'

'I'm sorry, gents, but I can't comment on that, I have my orders and I have told you as much as I dare. Like it or not...that's the position,' confirmed George.

'Hardly what you would call a sense of justice is it?' responded John indignantly.

'No, but it is a sense of compromise,' reflected Mike. 'As we said earlier, politics is a murky business, but sadly it seems that the impact of the bayonet will cast a very long shadow in this case.'

The four men sat calmly for a while then began chatting over some tea while the news sank in.

'Where does all this leave you, George?' enquired Mike.

'I'm not sure yet, but I'm due to be replaced shortly by Major Llewellyn Michael of the Welsh Guards and I've started thinking about retirement, can't be that far off,' replied George.

'There's plenty of beach to walk on here George. Membership of the gang can be negotiated you know,' responded Mike with a smile. 'Anyway you mentioned both good and bad news, so what's the good news?'

'Yes indeed! The good news. I did arrange for some tidying up on your behalf and a local ex army large car dealer who does a lot of business with the military heard of your mishap John and has stepped in. He's offered you a simple small car replacement free of charge and will scrap your old one to save you seeing the awful mess it's in. Mike, your villa has been tidied up and actually most of the impact was just a mess presumably for effect and not much actual damage was done, so it certainly isn't as bad as it must have seemed. Anyway it's reasonably back together now. And Paul...as it happens when I leave Cyprus I'm uncertain where I'm going and as my dog Misty has lived here all her life, I thought I'd leave her here in your safe keeping, if that's alright with you? She's a four year old black Labrador incidentally.'

The three men were quite astounded by this outbreak of kindness and generosity in what had appeared to be a sea of grot. Paul could almost sense tears in his eyes. They all expressed their gratitude and appreciation, although they couldn't help also wonder whether this was more to do with a sense of guilt on George's part or indeed an inducement to keep quiet, but it was never the less welcome.

After George had left, the three friends were at least reassured to hear that Markou was perceived to no longer see them as a threat and that George had arranged transport for them back to Cyprus tomorrow.

'I actually feel for Steve Mantel in these circumstances, he's been hung out to dry,' remarked Mike.

'Mike, don't forget the other possibility that he did in fact do it,' Paul reminded him.

'Yes, but it's the fact that in all this Markou, the slimy bastard, just walks away that really rankles.'

'Yes, there is that,' acknowledged Paul.

The three men started to think towards the future and to rebuilding their lives. It seemed unlikely that they would be required to give evidence in court, but felt they should explain to Anya what had happened, which might assist the cause of justice a little. That, they hoped would close their involvement in the affair, after helping George to deal with Mason of course.

Chapter 17

Anya was pleased to hear from Mike when he rang to arrange to go to see her.

'I had been concerned. I had heard about what happened to your villa and to the others then no one had heard anymore about you all; I was worried. I'm so pleased to hear that you are all OK.'

Mike was surprised by her concern. 'Anya, we want to come to see you to explain our position. We may be able to help you prepare your case but do not anticipate being called to court and for obvious reasons want to maintain a low profile.'

'Yes, of course, I understand. I would welcome that. How about tomorrow, Saturday morning will be quiet, say 10am?'

Mike agreed.

The three men arrived at the office in John's replacement car. It had been a very welcome offer from the car dealer. It was an older car, but nevertheless a workable means of transport and that was all John wanted. Anya greeted them warmly and invited them into her office. 'It's good to see that you are OK,' she said.

'Does that mean you thought we might not have been OK;, that Markou might have gone further?' replied Mike.

'I suppose so. I can't prove it but there have been people who have disappeared who you would reasonably judge to be in Markou's interests.'

Mike brought Anya up to date with developments as far as the three men were concerned.

'It looks like a stitch up really. Mantel could well have done it, but the authorities don't seem to be considering any other possibilities,' commented Paul.

'Yes, minds have been set from the start. I've seen Steve and agreed to represent him, but the evidence as it stands is pretty solidly against him and I have to agree that the system is likely to reap its revenge for the loss of one of its own.'

There was a call from reception that Major Cunningham had arrived to hand over some of Mantel's personal effects. Anya had not been expecting him, but was happy to pass the property over to Steve, or indeed to store it for him. George knocked on the door.

'Good morning, Miss Jabour, gentlemen; I thought I'd take the opportunity of handing over some of this personal kit; the Army would only destroy it otherwise.'

An irony thought John, like they were prepared to destroy Mantel himself.

'Major, I will take responsibility for this property and see to it that my client receives it in due course,' Anya agreed. 'I am however disappointed in your Army's attitude, Major, how easily you cast aside a man who has fought for your interests. There are no medals for the actions Steve Mantel took here in Cyprus, but for a young man he displayed extraordinary courage and integrity and we should recognise those qualities. I can't condone the killing, whatever happened that night, but his intensions and actions to aid civilian refugees were never the less admirable. So was his wish to challenge a man that the legitimate authorities choose to protect rather than expose. What is about to happen here is not justice Major, not for the victim or the people of Cyprus, or any other citizens of the world; it is a travesty and a tragedy.'

Major Cunningham was rather at a loss how to reply to this woman, so small in stature but so powerful in her presentation and conviction. He felt drawn; part of him could almost agree with her, but he could also see the wider picture and the need to protect wider political interests. As a soldier he accepted that his profession were generally only deployed when the politicians had failed and that the pursuit of wider goals usually cost lives. This however was somewhat different. Mantel had overstepped the mark, no doubt by trying to take the law into his own hands, but whether he genuinely deserved what was coming to him was questionable he acknowledged privately.

Silence fell before the Major took his leave. He had decided not to make any vain attempt at justifying the official position, as nobody was likely to be remotely impressed. John, Paul and Mike decided it was also best if they left, but before doing so John complemented Anya saying, 'Anya, well said. I think he almost agreed with you. You are obviously your own woman. '

'Yes, I am. I'm also a guest here, an immigrant. I know what that's like,' Anya replied.

'So do I,' added Paul.

'Actually, we are we all immigrants here in Cyprus,' added John.

Paul explained about his Polish roots and how his father had described being positively welcomed in England but that he had a mixed experience of being perceived as foreign.

'Yes, but you are white, Paul. Odd isn't it, after all this time that immigrants are still identified as different and people can be threatened by difference, and skin colour is such an obvious difference, it makes black immigrants standout even more... I happen to be black, a Muslim and a woman. I refuse to apologise for being any of these things, I am who I am. I choose to wear traditional Islamic dress, not out of fear, or cohesion or bigotry, but because it's part of me. I accept the argument and rational for having my face uncovered and I am happy to do so, but again because I've thought about it and I have adapted. I have chosen to do this because I think it's right, not because I'm expected to.'

The three men left with a growing respect for Anya. In the car park George was still there, he had waited for them and turned to say, 'By the way, I took on board your comments about Mason and have ordered him to see me at 08:30 on Monday morning in my office. It might help if you were present gentlemen as you know the full details of your evidence. I plan to confront him. I may not be able to influence matters as far as Mr Markou is concerned, but I can put my own house in order!'

The others all agreed and they parted quietly.

'So, one last throw of the dice then gents; Mason and then that's it,' commented Paul on the return journey in John's car.

'Yep, looks like it,' said John, as they all agreed.

****

Mason knocked firmly at the Major's door as expected, marched smartly in and saluted. He wasn't invited to sit down. Major Cunningham looked up. 'Ah Mason. You have met these three gentlemen?'

'Yes, Sir.'

'Mason, I'll come to the point. It comes to my attention that you may not be what you seem? These gentlemen have been subject to certain unwanted attentions recently which would have required access to certain military information and the link, to put it bluntly, appears to be you. I have trusted you Mason, you come and go through my office, attend to my guests and that makes you party to small parts of sensitive conversations. I appreciate that you are coming to the end of an unblemished army career and for that reason I have taken the unusual step of allowing this opportunity to explain yourself before I consider whether to take more formal action. So what have you got to say for yourself, man?' barked the Major.

'Bang to rights, Sir, you're correct,' answered Mason promptly.

'Is that it!' barked back the Major, dumbfounded.

'No, Sir.'

It transpired that Mason was actually an ex SAS man who was now working for MI6. He had been gathering intelligence on Stephan Markou for the last six months since arriving in Cyprus under this false identity. MI6 were concerned about Markou's activities and the potential to adversely influence events in Cyprus and impact negatively on civil/military relations, both with potential wider negative implications.

'Sir, I may as well be honest with you, my cover is blown here now and I'll be taken out of Cyprus immediately after this meeting. I have been monitoring Markou for some time and passing certain low level information to him in order to gain his trust,' Mason explained.

'So, let's get this right...that makes you...what, a sort of triple agent? said John, almost thinking aloud.

'If you like,' replied Mason.

'And you think on the basis of that, it was OK to effectively put us in danger, three retired British citizens!' demanded Mike.

'It's always a balance and a risk, but I feel I only really gave him information that he would have had access to anyway and my input played little part in what happened to you.'

'The ends justify the means, sort of thing?' interjected Paul.

'Sort of,' responded Mason.

'So what now? What about Markou and more to the point, what about Steve Mantel?' demanded Mike, sensing a collar.

'Markou, I'm afraid has friends in very high places and we haven't got enough on him yet to move against him, but give it time. Mantel I'm afraid is expendable. He stuck his nose in it where he shouldn't have.'

'You mean you set him up?' asked John.

'No. He was responsible for his own demise... ever since that ridiculous recce.'

'Recce? What recce?' retorted the Major quickly.

'Mantel and his side kicks decided to go freelance and seek to observe Markou's illegal people trafficking activities. I was on the ground too, watching them, watching Markou. From that point Mantel was in serious trouble. People tried to warn him, but he ignored their advice. Sorry, but that's how it goes,' replied Mason.

'I didn't know about this! Why wasn't I told?' demanded the Major, indignantly.

'You didn't need to know at the time, Sir, I'm sorry.'

'So you are not going to lobby on his behalf?' asked John.

'No. Not MI6's role... If he had killed Markou, then it might have been different, but to kill his henchman was really bad judgment.'

'Do you know that?' asked Mike.

'Not exactly. Markou had recorded events in the back room, as you suspected Chief Inspector, but the images were fairly inconclusive. The man certainly died as a result of the altercation, but exactly who held the knife at the time is debatable.'

'What about the DNA evidence?'

'Now come on Chief Inspector!'

'And the tape?'

'Markou had the tape in his possession when I saw him; he asked me to erase it in front of him, which I did, having switched it for a blank one while he was distracted.'

'You still have the tape?'

'Yes I do, and no you can't.'

****

So they were right in at least that Mason wasn't who they thought he was, although they didn't know and hadn't guessed his true identity. There had been some double dealing for 'wider purposes' and they were all going to have to live with the consequences.

John, Paul and Mike said their farewells and wished George good luck in the future, whatever that turned out to be after Cyprus and left the two soldiers to exchange stories before Mason disappeared into the murky background.

THE END

Epilogue

The following day John, Paul, Mike and Misty returned to the same table where they had first met at The Beach Bar. Long service in criminal justice had taught them all that things weren't always as they seemed and are seldom straight forward. Compromise becomes inevitable and sometimes that leaves justice in second place.

George Constantinou retired with due civil pomp and ceremony to enjoy a generous pension.

Major George Cunningham, the Rifles, was informed by the Brigadier that his retirement had been brought forward and that he was not required to serve a further last posting.

Stephan Markou continued his activities and his prominent, respectable local position.

Steve Mantel started a life sentence in a UK Category A prison.

And Rasha Ammar waits...

****

COMING SOON from Chris Boult

Out of the Shadow
The sequel to *In the Shadow of the Bayonet*

The cell door opened and Steve Mantel walked in to start his life sentence. It felt very strange. Thoughts took him back to the scene at the Sun Strip Bar, the stabbing, the bayonet and the injustice. He would never be a soldier again and it would be years until he could see former mates from The Parachute Regiment. The cell was small, but adequate, perversely far better equipped than his bed space in Camp Bastion in Afghanistan had been. He thought of his family, of initial training and selection, of war and of politics. He remembered mates who hadn't made it back and those that would never be the same.

Steve was about to enter a new world, one that was unfamiliar and one for which he was ill prepared. His uniform had changed to dull prison issue and his status from private soldier to prisoner, both as it happened with a number. He was however proud of one number and not the other. Not that he necessarily regretted the actions that had brought him here; he regretted how they had turned out, but not his intension to expose a far more serious and dangerous 'criminal' than himself. That had been laudable and hanging on to that thought was important to him. Yes a man had died, but another, Stefan Markou had escaped.

Steve Mantel had served with distinction in the British Army, but then had been convicted of the murder of a civilian in a Cypriot court and sentenced to life imprisonment, to be served in a UK jail. As an ex soldier he was used to discipline, to order and routine and to being 'processed', but all of that in his past life was to serve a certain purpose. In this new context although many of those features remained, there purpose was much more nebulous; to pass time, to punish, supposedly to rehabilitate. It had seemed like a long journey from Cyprus that had taken him to HMP Ashcourt, a Category A, high security prison in England, where he had experienced initial reception. The staff he found were, by and large firm but reasonable, given the context. In fact he couldn't help feel that this was in fact a military exercise, or indeed for real; that he had been captured and at any time now the punishment, interrogation and torture would start. He had been taught resistance to interrogation techniques and was trying to focus on the mental preparation to endure what was to come. Ironically, as he was to discover, in many ways this was to be a period of torture, but not short, violet and concentrated, but prolonged, slow and much more subtle. His ability to resist and to confront some demons were about to be tested to the full... and the journey would be a long one.

Lightning Source UK Ltd.
Milton Keynes UK
UKOW01f2229041117
312134UK00006B/271/P